The Obelisk

E.M. Forster

Modern Voices
Published by Hesperus Press Limited
4 Rickett Street, London SW6 1RU
www.hesperuspress.com

First published in 1972
First published by Hesperus Press Limited, 2009

Copyright © The Provost and Scholars of King's College, Cambridge 2009
Foreword © Amit Chaudhuri, 2009

Designed and typeset by Fraser Muggeridge studio
Printed in Jordan by the Jordan National Press

ISBN13: 978-1-84391-436-5

Contents

Foreword

These are extraordinarily funny and revealing and persuasive stories, concerning English manners, propriety, and appearances in the colonial world, and their being compromised by sex and low impulses and desires. That, in itself, is not a new theme: Kipling offered a brilliant diagnosis of such a situation as early as 1888, in his brief tale 'A Wayside Comedy', where a few English people who find themselves in an obscure hillside town in India manage to make history and the universe around them seem negligible in comparison to the narrative of their own deceptions and liaisons. Colonisation had a strange effect; it transported people to far-off places; it made the colonial, in his new habitat, seem at once emblematic and larger-than-life, and it also cocooned him and his family in a false Edenic calm – the calm of the expatriate ruling bourgeoisie – that is one of the most powerful fictions of colonialism. In that Eden (from whose vantage point the rest of the world principally constituted a problem of governance), the colonial and his wife were doomed to fall – from god-like control, Adamic innocence, or Eve-like susceptibility – again and again; through some minor but unseemly misdemeanour; through, often, embarrassingly, sex. Kipling describes the nature of that Eden, the microcosm contained within it, and the constant expectancy of danger in a handful of sentences in 'A Wayside Comedy':

> There are no amusements, except snipe and tiger shooting... Boulte, the Engineer, Mrs Boulte, and Captain Kurrell... are the English population of Kashima, if we except Major Vansuythen, who is of no importance whatsoever, and Mrs Vansuythen, who is the most important of us all... There was deep peace in Kashima till Mrs Vansuythen arrived.

The idyll, the 'deep peace', of the non-Western world, then, was agitated once and for all not only by the arrival on its shores of those two great missions, Christianity and Western civilisation, but of sex. Sex compromised those two missions, with their attendant moralities and pieties, from within. But it also did other things. It gave to the colonised world, partly, its misplaced sense of urgency and adventure; it inverted elements of the landscape, making small seem large, big appear inconsequential, secret trysts seem more pressing and absolute than historical pacts. Donne, writing in the heat of English expansionism, had sensed the comedy of inversions that sex wrought upon territorialism, where 'one little room' became an 'everywhere', and sex itself an epoch-marking voyage: 'O my new found land!'

These stories by Forster, in many ways, continue and consolidate that ironical, comic tradition, of making sex function, resiliently, as a narrative device at once expressing, dramatising, and undermining colonisation and conquest; and, through sex, bringing to the colonial protagonist what the administration, a higher authority, conscience, the colonised, or travel could not: an intimation of crisis and shame. The stories are full, too, of metaphors of the forms and genres of interaction that shaped the late nineteenth and early twentieth centuries, and through which strangers and classes (and, crucially, cultures) came into sudden contact with one another in a way that strained decorum and even credulity: excursions, tourist expeditions, an afternoon spent in a country house, a cruise. All these innocent, even genteel, activities, are, in this tradition, weighted, and fraught with the possibility of disrepute and scandal; with the possibility, really, of confronting utter strangeness – the end of civility. In a novel, they'd take up a chapter or episode (often of great significance), as they did in Forster's; in these stories, we are allowed to dwell a little longer as readers on how much of the episode in question was meant to draw attention to itself as construct, and how much pass off as reportage.

In one all-important sense, of course, these stories represent a departure from the classic type that 'A Wayside Comedy' consists of: their subject is not only the subterranean incursion of sex in the colonial enterprise (the stories becoming accounts, as a result, of subversion), but – and this is achieved with a striking candidness and an almost shocking equanimity – of sexuality; they are really studies, thus, of dislocation. The problem of sexuality gives to these stories – perhaps to all of Forster's mature fiction – its modernist disquiet, its obsession with duplication, alterity, otherness, and with echoes. The echo would lead to a profound crisis of revaluation in *A Passage to India*; and the echo is very much present in these stories too, asking the question, interrogating memory, as Adela Quested was cross-examined in the courtroom till she realised she'd got it wrong. So, in 'Dr Woolacott', a young man who is ill imagines he's had a romantic and sexual interlude with the man working outside, until he begins to wonder if the entire episode was a fantasy:

'... And when the others came in and opened the cupboard: your muscular and intelligent farmhand, your saviour from Wolverhampton in his Sunday suit – was he there?'

'No, he was not,' the boy sobbed.

'No, he was not,' came an echo, 'but perhaps I am here.'

Again, in 'Arthur Snatchfold', as the first moment of attraction is registered and noted (here, the recipient of attention has temporarily disappeared after a flirtation), so is the intimation of disjunction, the unsettling presence of the echo: 'Where had he gone off to now, he and his voice?... What was his name? Was he a local? Sir Richard put these questions to himself as he dressed.' Later, Sir Richard will hear from one of his peers how that young man who worked at the house he was visiting, and with whom he had an encounter mutually relished, was spotted by a policeman and prosecuted, but could not reveal who his anonymous, well-to-do lover was. The terrified Sir Richard nevertheless remembers what his partner-in-crime was called: 'Arthur Snatchfold. He had only heard the name once, and he would never hear it again.'

In *A Passage to India*, the echo ('ou-boum') was India and its infinite intractability; it undermined the name, and, with it, English identity (the sympathetic Mrs Moore's name is translated, by the 'native' crowd chanting outside the courtroom, into another echo: Esmiss Esmoor). Here, in these stories, we see what's arraigning Englishness is the otherness contained within desire; it takes the recognised symbols of that Englishness – names; even monuments, such as an obelisk in a seaside town – and either turns them into syllables, or puts them on hold, in abeyance, and subjects them to deferral: the obelisk is never actually seen; Dr Woolacott, after whom the story is named, is not an actual character in that story. This is akin to a Beckettian sense of the absurd, linked to Forster's delineation of the absurd in a British civilisational mission seen through the prism of a constantly present, but constantly suppressed, sexuality. In the longest story in this collection, 'The Other Boat', the result of the disgrace of homosexuality is the protagonist Lionel March's complete obliteration – not only the physical obliteration of his suicide, but a disintegration of the Englishness that was embodied in his identity: his mother 'never mentioned his name again'.

– *Amit Chaudhuri, 2009*

The Obelisk

Ernest was an elementary schoolmaster, and very very small; it was like marrying a doll, Hilda sometimes thought, and one with glass eyes too. She was larger herself: tall enough to make them look funny as they walked down the esplanade, but not tall enough to look dignified when she was alone. She cherished aspirations; none would have guessed it from her stumpy exterior. She yearned for a trip in a Rolls-Royce with a sheikh, but one cannot have everything or anything like it, one cannot even always be young. It is better to have a home of one's own than to always be a typist. Hilda did not talk quite as she should, and her husband had not scrupled to correct her. She had never forgotten – it was such a small thing, yet she could not forget it – she had never forgotten that night on their honeymoon when she had said something ungrammatical about the relative position of their limbs.

He was now asking her to decide whether they should sit in the shelter or walk to the obelisk. There was time to do one or the other before the bus went, but not to do both.

'Sit down will be best,' she replied. But as soon as they were in the shelter, looking at the undersized and under-coloured sea, she wished she had chosen the obelisk. 'Where is it? What's it for? Who's it to?' she asked.

'I don't know to whom it was erected – to some local worthy, one presumes. As regards its situation, it stands above the town in the direction of the landslip.'

'Would *you* like to go to it?'

'I can't honestly say that I should. My shoes are somewhat tight.'

'Yes, I suppose we're best where we are and then some tea. Do you know how far off it is?'

'I can't say that I do.'

'It may be quite near. Perhaps you could ask these people.' She lowered her voice, not to be overheard by the people in question: two sailors who were seated on the other side of the glass screen.

'I don't think I could well do that,' said Ernest timidly; a martinet at home and at school, he was terrified of anything unfamiliar.

'Why not?'

'They won't know.'

'They might.'

'There is no naval station here, Hilda, they are merely visitors like ourselves, no ships are ever stationed at a small watering-place.' He breathed on his pince-nez, and placed it between himself and the sea.

'Shall I ask them?'

'Certainly, if you wish to do so.'

Hilda opened her mouth to speak to the sailors, but no sound came out of it. 'You ask, it seems better,' she whispered.

'I don't wish to ask, I shall not ask, I have told you my reasons already, and if you are incapable of following them I really can do no more.'

'Oh all right, dear, don't get in such a fuss, it doesn't matter, I'm sure I don't want to go to your obelisk.'

'Why, in that case, do you want to inquire how to get there? And why "my" obelisk? I was not aware that I possessed one.'

She felt cross – Ernest did tie one up so – and determined to speak to the sailors to prove her independence. She had noticed them as she sat down, one of them particularly. 'Please excuse me,' she began. They were laughing at something, and did not hear her. 'Please could you kindly tell us – ' No reply. She got up and said to her husband, 'Oh, let's go, I hate this place.'

'Certainly, certainly,' said he, and they moved off down the esplanade in an offended silence. Hilda, who had been in the wrong, soon felt ashamed of herself. What on earth had made her behave like that, she wondered; it had been almost a quarrel, and all about nothing. She determined never to mention the beastly obelisk again.

This was not to be, for it appeared on a noticeboard, 'To the Obelisk and Landslip', and an arrow pointed to a gap in the crumbly cliffs. She would have marched by, but Ernest stopped. 'I think I should – I think I *should* like to go if you don't object,' he said, in a voice that was intended to be conciliatory. 'I could talk to the class about it on Monday. I am very short of material.'

Turning back, she looked at the shelter where they had sat. She could see the long dark legs of the sailors sticking out of it; the esplanade was almost deserted otherwise. 'No, of course I shouldn't mind,' she said.

'Excellent, excellent, admirable.' He led the way. The sea, such as it was, disappeared, and they began climbing a muddly sort of gorge – not romantic, though she tried to pretend it was so. Rocks of no great size overhung them, a stream dripped through mud. The weather was stuffy and an aeroplane could be heard being sick in the distance. Hilda took a stern line with herself; whatever they did this afternoon, she wanted to be doing something else. How nice Ernest was really! How genuine! How sincere! If only his forehead wasn't quite so bulgy, and had a little more hair hanging over it, if his shoes weren't quite so small and yellow, if he had eyes like a hawk and an aquiline nose and a sinewy sunburnt throat... no, no, that was asking too much, she must keep within bounds, she must not hope for a sinewy throat, or for reckless arms to clasp her beyond redemption... That came of going to those cinemas...

'It's ever so lovely here, don't you think,' she exclaimed, as they rounded a corner and saw a quantity of unripe blackberries.

'I should scarcely describe it in those terms.'

'I'm ever so glad we didn't stick in that awful shelter.'

'What makes you keep on saying "ever so"?'

'Oh, I'm sorry. Did I? Ever so what oughtn't I to have said?'

'No, no, you are getting it wrong. "Ever so what" is not the question, but "ever so" itself. The phrase is never needed. I can't think why it has become so popular. It is spreading into circles where one would not expect to hear it. Curious. You try to form a sentence in which "ever so" is not redundant.'

She tried, but her thoughts went off to that disastrous night when he had pulled her up in much the same way, and had made her feel worthless, and had humiliated her, and had afterwards tried to caress her, and she couldn't stand it. That had been his fault, but it was her fault if she minded now, she wanted to be really educated, and here he was helping her. Penitent, she looked at his pink and pear-shaped face, slightly beaded with sweat and topped by too small a hat, and determined to improve her grammar and to really love him.

There was a scrambling noise behind, and the two sailors came rushing up the path like monkeys.

'What do these fellows want here? I don't like this,' cried Ernest.

Stopping dead short, they smiled, showing dazzling teeth. One of them – not the one she had noticed – said, 'We right for the Oboblisk, chum?'

Ernest was nervous. The place was deserted, the path narrow, and he wouldn't anywhere have been easy with people whose bodies were so different from his own. He replied with more than his usual primness: 'Obelisk. The notice on the esplanade says "To the Obelisk and Landslip". I fear I can tell you no more.'

'Call it the Ob and be done, eh!'

'Thank you, sir, thank you, and thank you, madam,' said the other sailor. He was a much better type – an educated voice and a gallant bearing, and when Hilda stood aside to let them stride past he saluted her. 'Excuse us, sir,' he called back, as if the path and indeed the whole gorge was Ernest's private property.

'Sorry to trouble you, but we thought we'd go a walk, make the most of our brief time on shore, sir, you know.'

'A sensible thing to do,' said Ernest, who was recovering from his alarm, and liked being called sir.

'Just a little change, anyhow. Got a fag on you, Tiny?'

The other sailor fumbled in his jumper. 'Fergot 'em again,' he replied.

'Well, of all the…'

'Ferget me own what d'ye call 'em next.'

'Nice person to go out with, isn't he, sir? Promised to bring along a packet, then lets us both down!'

'Have one of mine if it comes to that,' said Ernest.

'No, sir, I won't do that, but it's very good of you all the same.'

'Oh, come along, my man, take one.'

'No, sir; I don't cadge.'

'Oh!' said Ernest, rather taken aback.

'Do have one, my husband has plenty.'

'No, thank you, madam, I'd rather not.' He had pride and a will, and a throb of pleasure went through her, pleasure mixed with despair. She felt him looking at her, and turned away to inspect the blackberries. In a moment he would go on, dart up the path with his companion, and disappear as it were into heaven.

'What about you?' said Ernest to the sailor so strangely called Tiny.

Tiny had no such scruples. He thrust out his huge paw with a grin and a grunt. 'Her' sailor shook his head and looked a little disdainful. 'There's nothing Tiny wouldn't say no to, is there, Tiny?' he remarked.

'Tiny's a sensible fellow,' said Ernest. The sailors, by their civil yet cheerful demeanour, had quite reassured him. He now dominated the situation, and behaved as if he was conducting an open-air class for older boys. 'Come along, Tiny.' He stretched up a match to the expectant lips.

'Thanks ever so,' Tiny responded.

Hilda let out a cackle. It was 'ever so', the forbidden phrase. The sailors laughed too, as did Ernest. He had become unusually genial. He astonished her by saying, 'Oh Hilda, I'm so sorry, here I am smoking and I never asked you whether you would smoke too.' It was the first time he had invited her to smoke in public. She declined, thinking he was testing her, but he asked her again and she took one.

'I'm ever so – I'm very sorry.'

'That's quite all right, dear, might I have a match?'

'Her' sailor whipped a box out of his breast. Tiny, equally polite, blew on the tip of his cigarette and held it towards her. She felt flustered, enmeshed in blue arms, dazzled by rose-red and sunburnt flesh, intoxicated by strength, saltiness, the unknown. When she escaped it was to her husband. Her sailor still held out the lighted match which she had used. 'Sir, may I change my mind and have one of your cigarettes after all?' he said coolly.

'Of course, of course, come along all and sundry.'

He took one, used the lighted match on it, then blew the match out and placed it in his breast. The match they had shared – there it lay… close to him, hidden in him, safe… He looked at her, touched his jumper, smiled a little and looked away, puffing his cigarette. At that moment the sun blazed out and it turned into a nice afternoon.

She looked away too. There was something dangerous about the man, something of the bird of prey. He had marked her down for his fell purpose, she must be careful like any other heroine. If only he wasn't so handsome, so out-of-the-way handsome. 'Who's saying no, Stan, now?' his companion guffawed. So his name was Stan… Stanley perhaps. What had led such a man to join the Navy? Perhaps some trouble at home.

'Stan's sensible, don't you tease Stan,' piped Ernest. They proceeded in a safe enough formation towards the Obelisk, the two sailors in front, she behind Tiny's buttocks, from which she had nothing to fear. Gradually the order altered – Ernest's fault. He was elated with his success, and kept on pestering the men with questions about their work. Tiny fell back to deal with them, but was ill-informed. So 'Stan' joined them, and she went on ahead. It was nicer than she expected – everyone good-tempered, including her husband. But she still wished she had not come.

'It's a funny thing, a day on shore,' said the easy silky voice. He had stolen up behind her – no scrambling this time. She turned, and his eyes moved up and down her body.

'How do you mean, funny? I don't understand.'

'You hardly know what to do with yourself. You're let out of prison, as it were, the discipline stops, you find a shipmate who happens to be on leave too, you go off with him, though you have nothing in common, he wants to go to the pictures, so you go, he thinks he'd like a walk, so you go, he asks the way of strangers, with the result that you inflict yourself on them too. It's a funny life, the Navy. You're never alone, you're never independent. I don't like tacking on to people, the way that youngster I'm with does. I've told him of it before, but he turns everything into a joke.'

'Why is he called Tiny?'

'Merely because he's so large. Another joke. You know the kind of thing, and how weary one gets of it. Still, life's not a bed of roses anywhere, I suppose.'

'No, it isn't, it isn't.'

She ought not to have made such a remark, and she was glad when he ignored it and went on, 'And I've got to be called Stan although my name's really Stanhope.'

'Stanhope?'

'It was my mother's family name. We came from Cheshire. However, all that's over, and I'm Stan.' There was a tinge of melancholy in his voice which made it fatally attractive. For all his gaiety, he had suffered, suffered… When she threw away her cigarette he did the same and he gently touched his breast.

This frightened Hilda. She didn't want any nonsense, and she suggested that they should wait for her husband. He obeyed, and turned his profile to her as they waited. He looked even finer that way than full face; the brow was so noble, the nose and the chin so fine, the lips so tender, the head poised so beautifully upon the sinewy neck, the colouring lovelier than imagination can depict. Here, however, was Ernest, coming round the corner like a cheerful ant. He held Tiny's cap in his hand, and was questioning him on the subject of his naval costume.

'Are we going on any further?' she called.

'I think so. Why not?'

'It seems turning out rather a climb.'

'We have plenty of time, abundance of time, before the bus goes.'

'Yes, but we must be keeping these gentlemen back, you and I walk so slowly.'

'I was not aware of walking slowly. You in a hurry, Stan?' he called familiarly.

'Not the least, not in the very least, sir, thank you.'

'You, Tiny?'

'Hurry for what?'

'Do you want to go on and leave us?'

Grateful to Hilda for calling him a gentleman, he beamed up at her and said, 'What's 'is name, please?' – pointing to Ernest as if he were some rare animal and could not answer questions.

'My husband – his name's Ernest.'

'Think his trilby'd fit me?' His hand shot out to pull it off, but he was checked by a quiet word of reproof from Stanhope. Ernest scuttled back a step. 'Chum, I won't hurt you, chum, chuck chuck, chum, chum,' as if feeding chicken.

'Certain people always go too far, they spoil things, it's a pity,' Stanhope remarked to her as they continued their walk.

How right he was – though for the moment Tiny had entertained her, also she got a wicked pleasure when Ernest's cowardice got exposed. She smiled, and felt clever herself, not realising that Stanhope now walked behind her, which was exactly what she had not meant to happen. 'My husband and him seem getting on quite nicely,' she said.

'Tiny's always ready to play the fool, day in, day out. I'm afraid I don't understand it. Something wrong with me, I suppose.'

'One gets rather tired of anything that's always the same, I think.'

He offered no opinion, and they walked on for five minutes without saying anything. The path was well marked and not steep, and many pretty flowers, both yellow and pink, grew between the stones. Glimpses of the sea appeared, dancing blue, the aeroplane turned into a gull. The interval separating the two sailors gradually increased. 'What made you join the Navy?' she said suddenly.

He told her – it was fascinating. He was of good family – she had guessed as much! – but wanted to see the world. He had left a soft job in an office when he was eighteen. He told her the name of the office. She happened to have heard of it in her typist days, and was instantly possessed by a feeling of security. Of course she was safe with him – ridiculous. He reeled off the names of ports, known and unknown. He was not very young when you were close to him, but Hilda did not like very young men, they were not distinguished, and her dream was distinction. These well-marked features, this hair, raven-black against the snowy line of the cap, yet flecked at the temples with grey, suited her best, oh and those eyes, cruel eyes, kind eyes, kind, cruel, oh! they burnt into your shoulders, if you turned and faced them it was worse. And she so dumpy! She tried to steady herself by her modesty, which was considerable, and well-grounded. And a batch of people came downhill and passed them – it was only an extension of the esplanade. 'No, Hilda, no one like this is going to bother to seduce you,' she told herself.

'I suppose I can't persuade you,' he said. He took out of his jumper a cigarette case, and opened it.

'But I thought you hadn't got any cigarettes,' she cried.

He snapped the case up, put it back, and said, 'Caught!'

'What do you mean? Why ever did you ask for one when you had all those?'

'I decline to answer that question,' he smiled.

'I want to know. You must answer. Tell me! Oh, go on! Do tell me.'

'No, I won't.'

'Oh, you're horrid.'

'Am I? Why?' The ravine had got wilder, almost beautiful. The path climbed above thick bushes and little trees. She knew they ought to wait again for Ernest, but her limbs drove her on. She repeated, 'You must tell me. I insist.' He drove her more rapidly before him. Then he said, 'Very well, but promise not to be angry.'

'I'm angry with you already.'

'Then I may as well tell. I pretended I'd no cigarettes on the chance of your husband offering me one.'

'But why? You said no when he did.'

'It wasn't a cigarette that I wanted. And now I suppose you're angry. I didn't want to go on, and it was my only chance of stopping. So I asked Tiny for one. I knew he'd be out of them, he always is. I wanted to – ' He took the extinguished match from his pocket. 'Better throw this away now, hadn't I? Or you'll be angry again.'

'I'm not angry, but don't start being silly, please.'

'There are worse things than silliness.'

Hilda didn't speak. Her knees were trembling, her heart thumping, but she hurried on. Whether he threw the match away or not she did not know. After a pause he said in quite a different voice, 'I've done quite enough talking, you know. Now you talk.'

'I've nothing to say,' she said, her voice breaking. 'Nothing ever happens to me, nothing will, I… I do feel so odd.' He seemed to tug her this way and that. If only he wasn't so lovely! His hand touched her. Almost without her knowing, he guided her off the path, and got her down among the bushes.

Once there, she was lost. Under pretext of comforting he came closer. He persuaded her to sit down. She put her hand to his jersey to thrust him off, and it slid up to his throat. He was so gentle as well as so strong, that was the trouble, she did not know which way to resist him, and those eyes, appealing, devouring, appealing. He constrained her to lie down. A little slope of grass, scarcely bigger than a couch, was the scene of her inadequate resistance; beyond the dark blue of his shoulders she could see the blue of the sea, all around were thick thorny bushes covered with flowers, and she let him do what he wanted.

'Keep still,' he whispered. 'They're passing.'

From the path came the sound of feet.

'Don't talk just yet.' He continued to hold her, his chin raised, listening.

'They've gone now, but talk quietly. It's all right. He won't know. I'll fix up a story. Don't you worry. Don't you cry.'

'It's your fault, you made me…'

He laughed gently, not denying it. He raised her up, his arms slanting across her back unexpectedly kind. He let her say whatever she wanted to, as long as she did not say it too loud, and now and then he stroked her hair. She accused him, she exalted Ernest, repeating, 'I'm not what you think I am at all.'

All he said was 'That's all right,' or 'You shan't come into any trouble, I swear it, I swear it, and you mustn't cry,' or 'I play tricks – yes. But I never let a woman down. Look at me. Do as I tell you! Look at me, Hilda.'

She obeyed. Her head fell on his shoulder, and she gave him a kiss. For the first time in her life she felt worthy. Her humiliation slipped from her, never to return. She had pleased him.

'Stanhope…'

'Yes, I know.'

'What do you know?'

'I'm waiting until it's absolutely safe. Yes.'

He held her against him for a time, then laid her again on the grass. She was consciously deceiving her husband, and it was heaven. She took the lead, ordered the mysterious stranger, the film star, the sheikh, what to do, she was, for one moment, a queen, and he her slave. They came out of the depths together, confederates. He helped her up, then respectfully turned away. She hated grossness, and nothing he did jarred.

When they were back on the path, he laid his plan. 'Hilda, it's no use going on to the Obelisk,' he said, 'it's too late, they're in front of us and we shall meet them coming down. He'll want to know how they passed us without seeing us, and if you've an explanation of that I've not. No. We shall have to go back and wait for them on the esplanade.'

She patted her hair – she had good hair.

'Make up some story when they arrive. Muddle them. We shall never muddle them if we meet them face to face on this path. You leave it to me – I'll confuse them in no time.'

'But how?' she said dubiously, as they started the long descent.

'I shall see when I see them. That's how I always work.'

'Don't you think it would be better if you hid here, and I went down alone? Our bus leaves before very long, then you'll be safe.'

He shook his head, and showed his teeth, scorning her gaily. 'No, no, I'm better at telling stories than you, I don't trust you. Take your orders from me, don't ask questions and it'll be all right. I swear it will. We shall pull through.'

Yes, he was wonderful. She would have this gallantry to look back upon, especially at night. She could think of Ernest quite kindly, she'd be able to put up with him when he made his little wrong remarks or did his other little wrong things. She'd her dream, and what people said was false and what the Pictures said was true: it was worth it, worth being clasped once in the right arms, though you never had them round you again. She had got what she longed for, and it was what she longed for, not a smack in the face, not a sell... She had always yearned for a lover who would be nice *afterwards* – not turn away like a satisfied brute, as handsome men are supposed to do. Stanhope was – what do you call it... a gentleman, a knight in armour, a real sport... O for words. Her eyes filled with happy tears of happiness.

Swinging ahead of her on to the esplanade, he gave her his final instructions. 'Take your line from me, remember we've done nothing we shouldn't, remember it's going to be much easier than you think, and don't lose your head. Simpler to say than to do, all the same don't do it, and if you can't think of anything else to do look surprised. Our first job is to sit down quietly on the esplanade and wait.'

But they were not to wait. As they came out of the gap in the cliffs, they saw Ernest on a bench, and Tiny leaning on the esplanade railings observing the sea. Ernest jumped up all a bunch of nerves, crying, 'Hilda, Hilda, where have you been? Why weren't you at the Obelisk? We looked and looked for you there, we hunted all the way back –'

Before she could answer, indeed before he had finished, Stanhope launched a violent counter-attack. 'What happened to you, sir? We got up to the Obelisk and waited, then we've been shouting and calling all the way back. The lady's been so worried – she thought an accident had happened. Are you all right, sir?' He bayed on, full-chested, magnificent, plausible, asking questions and allowing no time for their reply.

'Hilda, impossible, you couldn't have been, or I should have seen you.'

'There we were, sir, we had a good look at the view and waited for you, and then came down. It was not meeting you on the way back that puzzled us so.'

'Hilda, were you really...'

By now she had had her cue, and she heard her voice a long way off saying in fairly convincing tones, 'Oh yes, we got up to the Obelisk.'

And he believed, or three-quarters believed her. How shocking, but what a respite! It was the first lie she had ever told him, and it was unlikely she would ever tell him a worse. She felt very odd – not ashamed, but so queer, and Stanhope went on with his bluffing. The wind raised his dark forelock and his collar. He looked the very flower of the British Navy as he lied and lied. 'I can't understand it,' he repeated. 'It's a relief to know nothing's wrong, but not to run into you as we came down... I don't understand it, I'm what you may call stumped, well, I'm damned.'

'I'm puzzled equally, but there is nothing to be gained by a prolonged discussion. Hilda, shall we go to our bus?'

'I don't want you to go until you feel satisfied,' said she. A false step; she realised as much as soon as she had spoken.

'Not satisfied? I am perfectly satisfied. With what have I to be dissatisfied? I only fail to grasp how I failed to find you when I reached the monument.'

Hilda dared not go away with him with things as they were. She didn't know how to work out the details of the lie, it was in too much of a lump. Alarmed, she took refuge in crossness. 'You've got to grasp it some time or other, you may as well now,' she snapped. Her lover looked at her anxiously.

'Well, be that as that may be, we must go.'

'What's your explanation, Tiny?' called Stanhope, in his splendid authoritative way, to create a diversion.

Tiny cocked up one heel and replied not.

'He can scarcely solve a problem which baffles the three of us, and it is so strange that you were ahead of us on the path going up, yet a good ten minutes behind us coming down,' enunciated Ernest.

'Come along, Tiny, you've a tongue in your head, haven't you, mate? I'm asking you a question. Don't stand there like a stuck pig.'

'Ber-yutiful view,' said Tiny, turning round and extending his huge blue arms right and left along the railings of the esplanade. 'You was showing the lady the Ob, perhaps.'

'Of course we inspected the monument. You know that. You haven't answered my question.'

''Ope you showed it 'er properly while you was about it, Stan. Don't do to keep a thing like that all to yourself, you know. Ern, why they call that an ob?'

'Obelisk, obelisk,' winced Ernest, and was evidently more anxious to go.

'You said it, obblepiss.'

'I said nothing of the sort.'

'You said it, obblepiss.' The giant was grinning amiably, and seemed totally unaware that anything had gone wrong. But how different sailors are! How unattractive, in Tiny's case, was the sun-reddened throat and the line of broad shoulders against the sea! He was terribly common, really, and ought not to be answering people back. 'Anyone ever seed a bigger one?' he inquired. No one replied, and how should they to so foolish a question? 'Stands up, don't it?' he continued. No one spoke. 'No wonder they call that a needle, for wouldn't that just prick.'

'Stop that infernal talk at once,' exploded Stanhope, and he seemed needlessly vexed, but oh, how handsome he looked, and how his dark eyes flashed; she was glad to see him angry and to have this extra memory.

'Stan, Stan, what's the matter, Stan?'

'If you speak again I'll brain you.'

'Ever seed a bigger one – a bigger obolokist, I mean. That's all I said. Because I 'ave. Killopatra's Needle's bigger. Well? Well? What you all staring at me for? What you think I was going to say? Eh? Oh, look at little Ern, ain't he just blushing. Oh, look at Stan. Lady, look at 'em.'

Hilda did observe that the two older men were going most extraordinary colours, her lover purplish, her husband rose-pink. And she did not like the tone of the conversation herself, she scarcely knew why, and feared something awkward might come out if it went on much longer. 'We must go, or we shall miss that bus,' she announced. 'We shall never clear up why we never met, and it isn't of the least importance. Ernest, do come along, dear.'

Ernest muttered that he was willing, and the episode ended. Goodbyes were said, by Tiny tempestuously. Plunging across the esplanade, he seized the unfortunate schoolmaster's arm, and whirled it around like a windmill. 'Goo bye, Ern, take care of yerself, pleased to have met yer, termater face and all,' he bawled.

'Pleased to have met you both,' said Ernest with restraint.

'Ju-jitsu... now as yer neck snaps...'

Hilda and Stanhope profited by this noisy nonsense to their farewells. They would not have dared otherwise. The touch of his hand was cool and dry, but he was nearly worn out, and it trembled. It had not been easy for him, returning her unreproached and unsuspected to her husband, fighting for her, using stratagem after stratagem, following hopeless hints… The perfect knight! The gangster lover who really cares, who knows… 'My darling… thank you for everything for ever,' she breathed. He dared not reply, but his lips moved, and he slipped his left hand into his breast. She knew what he meant: the match was there, the symbol of their love. He would never forget her. She had lived. She was saved.

What a contrast to the other – so boisterous, so common, so thoroughly unattractive! It was strange to think of them in the same uniform, strange to look down the esplanade and see them getting more and more like one another as the distance increased. The actual parting had gone off easily, Ernest had produced his cigarettes again. 'Have one more, both of you, before you repair to your boat,' he called. The powerfully made sailors stooped, the lean distinguished fingers and the battered clumsy ones helped themselves again to his bounty. Perky, he had lit up himself, and now he was strutting away with his good little wife on his arm.

Of course the first few minutes alone with him were awful. Still, she drew strength from the fact that she had deceived him so completely. And somehow she did not despise him, she did not despise him at all. He seemed nicer than usual, and she was pleased when he started to discuss the relative advantages of gas and electricity. He said one thing, she another, while the cloud of her past swept gloriously out to sea. Home and its details had a new freshness. Even when the night came, she should feel differently and not mind.

They reached the bus stop with several minutes to spare. There was a picture-postcard kiosk, and she had a good idea: she would buy a postcard of the Obelisk, so that if the topic came up again she would know what it looked like.

There was an excellent selection, and she soon visualised it from several points of view. Though not as tall as Cleopatra's

Needle, it boasted a respectable height. One of the cards showed the inscription 'Erected in 1879 to the memory of Alfred Judge, one-time Mayor'. She memorised this, for Ernest often mentioned inscriptions, but she actually bought a card which brought in some of its surroundings. The monument was nobly placed. It stood on a tongue of rock overlooking the landslip.

'Well, you won't have seen that today! Will you?' said the woman in the kiosk as she took payment.

Hilda thought she would fall to the ground. 'Oh gracious: whatever do you mean?' she gasped.

'It's not there to be seen.'

'But that's the Obelisk. It says so.'

'It says so, but it's not there. It fell down last week. During all that rain. It's fallen right over into the landslip upside down, the tip of it's gone in ever so far, rather laughable though I suppose it'll be a loss to the town.'

'Ah, there it is,' said her husband, coming up and taking the postcard out of her hand. 'Yes, it gives quite a good idea of it, doesn't it? I'll have one displaying the inscription.'

Then the bus swept up and took them away. Hilda sank into a seat nearly fainting. Depth beneath depth seemed to open. For if she couldn't have seen the Obelisk he couldn't have seen it either, if she had dawdled on the way up he must have dawdled too, if she was lying he must be lying, if she and a sailor – she stopped her thoughts, for they were become meaningless. She peeped at her husband, who was on the other side of the coach, studying the postcard. He looked handsomer than usual, and happier, and his lips were parted in a natural smile.

The Life to Come

Night

Love had been born somewhere in the forest, of what quality only the future could decide. Trivial or immortal, it had been born to two human bodies as a midnight cry. Impossible to tell whence the cry had come, so dark was the forest. Or into what worlds it would echo, so vast was the forest. Love had been born for good or evil, for a long life or a short.

There was hidden among the undergrowth of that wild region a small native hut. Here, after the cry had died away, a light was kindled. It shone upon the pagan limbs and the golden ruffled hair of a young man. He, calm and dignified, raised the wick of a lamp which had been beaten down flat, he smiled, lit it, and his surroundings trembled back into his sight. The hut lay against the roots of an aged tree, which undulated over its floor and surged at one place into a natural couch, a sort of throne, where the young man's quilt had been spread. A stream sang outside, a firefly relit its lamp also. A remote, a romantic spot… lovely, loveable… and then he caught sight of a book on the floor, and he dropped beside it with a dramatic moan as if it was a corpse and he the murderer. For the book in question was his Holy Bible. 'Though I speak with the tongues of men and of angels, and have not – 'A scarlet flower hid the next word, flowers were everywhere, even round his own neck. Losing his dignity, he sobbed 'Oh, what have I done?' and not daring to answer the question he hurled the flowers through the door of the hut and the Bible after them, then rushed to retrieve the latter in an agony of grotesque remorse. All had fallen into the stream, all were carried away by the song. Darkness and beauty, darkness and beauty. 'Only one end to this,' he thought. And he scuttled back for his pistol. But the pistol was not with him, for he was negligent in his arrangements and had left it over with the servants at the farther side of the great tree; and the servants, awoken from slumber, took alarm at his talk of firearms. In spite of all he could say, they concluded that an attack was impending from the neighbouring village, which had already proved unfriendly, and they implored their young master not to resist, but to hide in the brushwood until dawn and slip away as soon as the forest paths were visible. Contrary to his orders, they began packing and next morning he was riding away from the enchanted hut, and descending the watershed into the next valley. Looking back at the huge and enigmatic masses of the trees, he prayed them to keep his unspeakable secret, to conceal it even from God, and he felt in his unhinged state that they had the power to do this, and that they were not ordinary trees.

When he reached the coast, the other missionaries there saw at once from his face that he had failed. Nor had they expected otherwise. The Roman Catholics, far more expert than themselves, had failed to convert Vithobai, the wildest, strongest, most stubborn of all the inland chiefs. And Paul Pinmay (for this was the young man's name) was at that time a very young man indeed, and had partly been sent in order that he might discover his own limitations. He was inclined to be impatient and headstrong, he knew little of the language and still less of native psychology, and indeed he disdained to study this last, declaring in his naive way that human nature is the same all over the world. They heard his story with sympathy but without surprise. He related how on his arrival he had asked for an audience, which Vithobai had granted inside his ancestral stockade. There, dictionary in hand, he had put the case for Christ, and at the end Vithobai, not deigning to reply in person, had waved to a retainer and made him answer. The retainer had been duly refuted, but Vithobai remained impassive and unfriendly behind his amulets and robes. So he put the case a second time, and another retainer was put up against him, and the audience continued on these lines until he was so exhausted that he was fain to withdraw. Forbidden to sleep in the village, he was obliged to spend the night all alone in a miserable hut, while the servants kept careful watch before the entrance and reported that an attack might be expected at any moment. He had therefore judged it fitter to come away at sunrise. Such was his story – told in a mixture of missionary jargon and of slang – and towards the close he was looking at his colleagues through his long eyelashes to see whether they suspected anything.

'Do you advise a renewed attempt next week?' asked one of them, who was addicted to irony.

And another: 'Your intention, I think, when you left us, was to get into touch with this unapproachable Vithobai personally, indeed you declared that you would not return until you had done so.'

And a third: 'But you must rest now, you look tired.'

He was tired, but as soon as he lay down his secret stole out of its hiding place beyond the mountains, and lay down by his side. And he recalled Vithobai, Vithobai the unapproachable, coming into his hut out of the darkness and smiling at him. Oh how delighted he had been! Oh how surprised! He had scarcely recognised the sardonic chief in this gracious and bare-limbed boy, whose only ornaments were scarlet flowers. Vithobai had laid all formality aside. 'I have come secretly,' were his first words. 'I wish to hear more about this god whose name is Love.' How his heart had leapt after the despondency of the day! 'Come to Christ!' he had cried, and Vithobai had said, 'Is that your name?' He explained No, his name was not Christ, although he had the fortune to be called Paul after a great apostle, and of course he was no god but a sinful man, chosen to call other sinners to the Mercy Seat. 'What is Mercy? I wish to hear more,' said Vithobai, and they sat down together upon the couch that was almost a throne. And he had opened the Bible at I. Cor. 13, and had read and expounded the marvellous chapter, and spoke of the love of Christ and of our love for each other in Christ, very simply but more eloquently than ever before, while Vithobai said, 'This is the first time I have heard such words, I like them,' and drew closer, his body aglow and smelling sweetly of flowers. And he saw how intelligent the boy was and how handsome, and determining to win him there and then imprinted a kiss on his forehead and drew him to Abraham's bosom. And Vithobai had lain in it gladly – too gladly and too long – and had extinguished the lamp. And God alone saw them after that.

Yes, God saw and God sees. Go down into the depths of the woods and He beholds you, throw His Holy Book into the stream, and you destroy only print and paper, not the Word. Sooner or later, God calls every deed to the light. And so it was with Mr Pinmay. He began, though tardily, to meditate upon his sin. Each time he looked at it its aspect altered. At first he assumed that all the blame was his, because he should have set an example. But this was not the root of the matter, for Vithobai had shown no reluctance to be tempted. On the contrary... and it was his hand that beat down the light. And why had he stolen up from the village if not to tempt...? Yes, to tempt, to attack the new religion by corrupting its preacher, yes, yes, that was it, and his retainers celebrated his victory now in some cynical orgy. Young Mr Pinmay saw it all. He remembered all that he had heard of the antique power of evil in the country, the tale he had so smilingly dismissed as beneath a Christian's notice, the extraordinary uprushes of energy which certain natives were said to possess and occasionally to employ for unholy purposes. And having reached this point he found that he was able to pray; he confessed his defilement (the very name of which cannot be mentioned among Christians), he lamented that he had postponed, perhaps for a generation, the victory of the Church, and he condemned, with increasing severity, the arts of his seducer. On the last topic he became truly eloquent, he always found something more to say, and having begun by recommending the boy to mercy he ended by asking that he might be damned.

'But perhaps this is going too far,' he thought, and perhaps it was, for just as he finished his prayers there was a noise as of horsemen below, and then all his colleagues came dashing into his room. They were in extreme excitement. Cried one: 'News from the interior, news from the forest. Vithobai and the entire of his people have embraced Christianity.' And the second: 'Here we have the triumph of youth, oh it puts us to shame.' While the third exclaimed alternately 'Praise be to God!' and 'I beg your pardon.' They rejoiced one with another and rebuked their own hardness of heart and want of faith in the Gospel method, and they thought the more highly of young Pinmay because he was not elated by his success, on the contrary, he appeared to be disturbed, and fell upon his knees in prayer.

2

Evening

Mr Pinmay's trials, doubts and final triumphs are recorded in a special pamphlet, published by his Society and illustrated by woodcuts. There is a picture called 'What it seemed to be', which shows a hostile and savage potentate threatening him; in another picture, called 'What it really was!', a dusky youth in western clothes sits among a group of clergymen and ladies, looking like a waiter, and supported by under-waiters, who line the steps of a building labelled 'School'. Barnabas (for such was the name that the dusky youth received at his baptism) – Barnabas proved an exemplary convert. He made mistakes, and his theology was crude and erratic, but he never backslid, and he had authority with his own people, so that the missionaries had only to explain carefully what they wanted, and it was carried out. He evinced abundant zeal, and behind it a steadiness of purpose all too rare. No one, not even the Roman Catholics, could point to so solid a success.

Since Mr Pinmay was the sole cause of the victory, the new district naturally fell to his charge. Modest, like all sincere workers, he was reluctant to accept, refusing to go although the chief sent deputation after deputation to escort him, and only going in the end because he was commanded to do so by the Bishop. He was appointed for a term of ten years. As soon as he was installed, he set to work energetically – indeed, his methods provoked criticism, although they were fully justified by their fruits. He who had been wont to lay such stress on the Gospel teaching, on love, kindness, and personal influence, he who had preached that the Kingdom of Heaven is intimacy and emotion, now reacted with violence and treated the new converts and even Barnabas himself with the gloomy severity of the Old Law. He who had ignored the subject of native psychology now became an expert therein, and often spoke more like a disillusioned official than a missionary. He would say: 'These people are so unlike ourselves that I much doubt whether they have really accepted Christ. They are pleasant enough when they meet us, yet probably spread all manner of ill-natured gossip when our backs are turned. I cannot wholly trust them.' He paid no respect to local customs, suspecting them all to be evil, he undermined the tribal organisation, and – most risky of all – he appointed a number of native catechists of low type from the tribe in the adjoining valley. Trouble was expected, for this was an ancient and proud people, but their spirit seemed broken, or

Barnabas broke it where necessary. At the end of the ten years the Church was to know no more docile sons.

Yet Mr Pinmay had his anxious moments.

His first meeting with Barnabas was the worst of them.

He had managed to postpone it until the day of his installation by the Bishop, and of the general baptism. The ceremonies were over, and the whole tribe, headed by their chief, had filed past the portable font and been signed on the forehead with the cross of Christ. Mistaking the nature of the rite, they were disposed to gaiety. Barnabas laid his outer garment aside, and running up to the group of missionaries like any young man of his people said, 'My brother in Christ, oh come quickly,' and stroked Mr Pinmay's flushed face, and tried to kiss his forehead and golden hair.

Mr Pinmay disengaged himself and said in a trembling voice, 'In the first place send your people each to his home.'

The order was given and obeyed.

'In the second place, let no one come before me again until he is decently clad,' he continued, more firmly.

'My brother, like you?'

The missionary was now wearing a suit of ducks with shirt, vest, pants and cholera belt, also sun helmet, starched collar, blue tie spotted with white, socks, and brown boots. 'Yes, like me,' he said. 'And in the third place are you decently clad yourself, Barnabas?'

The chief was wearing but little. A cincture of bright silks supported his dagger and floated in the fresh wind when he ran. He had silver armlets, and a silver necklet, closed by a falcon's head which nestled against his throat. His eyes flashed like a demon, for he was unaccustomed to rebuke, but he submitted and vanished into his stockade.

The suspense of the last few weeks had quite altered Pinmay's character. He was no longer an open-hearted Christian knight but a hypocrite whom a false step would destroy. The retreat of Barnabas relieved him. He saw that he had gained an ascendancy over the chief which it was politic to develop. Barnabas respected him, and would not willingly do harm – had even an affection for him, loathsome as the idea might seem. All this was to the good. But he must strike a second blow. That evening he went in person to the stockade, taking with him two colleagues who had recently arrived and knew nothing of the language.

The chief received them in soiled European clothes – in the interval he had summoned one of the traders who accompanied the baptismal party. He had mastered his anger, and speaking courteously he said: 'Christ awaits us in my inner chamber.'

Mr Pinmay had thought out his line of action. He dared not explain the hideous error, nor call upon his fellow sinner to repent; the chief must remain in a state of damnation for a time, for a new church depended on it. His reply to the unholy suggestion was 'Not yet.'

'Why not yet?' said the other, his beautiful eyes filling with tears. 'God orders me to love you now.'

'He orders me to refrain.'

'How can that be, when God *is* Love?'

'I have served him the longer and I know.'

'But this is my palace and I am a great chief.'

'God is greater than all chiefs.'

'As it was in your hut let it here be. Dismiss your companions and the gate will be barred behind them, and we close out the light. My body and the breath in it are yours. Draw me again to your bosom. I give myself, I, Vithobai the King.'

'Not yet,' repeated Mr Pinmay, covering his eyes with his hand.

'My beloved, I give myself… take me… I give you my kingdom.' And he fell prone.

'Arise, Barnabas. We do not want your kingdom. We have only come to teach you to rule it rightly. And do not speak of what happened in the hut. Never mention the hut, the word hut, the thought, either to me or to anyone. It is my wish and my command.'

'Never?'

'Never.'

'Come, my gods, come back to me,' he cried, leaping and wrenching at his clothes. 'What do I gain by leaving you?'

'No, no no!' prevaricated Mr Pinmay. 'I said "Never speak", not that I would never come.'

The boy was reassured. He said, 'Yes. I misunderstood. You do come to Christ, but not yet. I must wait. For how long?'

'Until I call you. Meanwhile obey all my orders, whether given directly or through others.'

'Very well, my brother. Until you call me.'

'And do not call me your brother.'

'Very well.'

'Or seek my company.' Turning to the other missionaries, he said, 'Now let us go.' He was glad he had brought companions with him, for his repentance was still insecure. The sun was setting, the inner chamber garlanded, the stockade deserted, the boy wild with passion, weeping as if his heart had broken. They might have been so happy together in their sin and no one but God need have known.

3

Day

The next crisis that Mr Pinmay had to face was far less serious, yet it shocked him more, because he was unprepared for it. The occasion was five years later, just before his own marriage. The cause of Christ had progressed greatly in the interval. Dancing had been put down, industry encouraged, inaccurate notions as to the nature of religion had disappeared, nor in spite of espionage had he discovered much secret immorality. He was marrying one of the medical missionaries, a lady who shared his ideals, and whose brother had a mining concession above the village.

As he leant over the veranda, meditating with pleasure on the approaching change in his life, a smart European dog-cart drove up, and Barnabas scrambled out of it to pay his congratulations. The chief had developed into an affable and rather weedy Christian with a good knowledge of English. He likewise was about to be married – his bride a native catechist from the adjoining valley, a girl inferior to him by birth, but the missionaries had selected her.

Congratulations were exchanged.

Mr Pinmay's repentance was now permanent, and his conscience so robust that he could meet the chief with ease and transact business with him in private, when occasion required it. The brown hand, lying dead for an instant in his own, awoke no reminiscences of sin.

Wriggling rather awkwardly inside his clothes, Barnabas said with a smile: 'Will you take me a short drive in your dog cart, Mr Pinmay?'

Mr Pinmay replied that he had no dog cart.

'Excuse me, sir, you have. It stands below. It, and the horse, are my wedding gift to you.'

The missionary had long desired a horse and cart, and he accepted them without waiting to ask God's blessing. 'You should not have given me such an expensive present,' he remarked. For the chief was no longer wealthy; in the sudden advent of civilisation he had chanced to lose much of his land.

'My reward is enough if we go one drive, sir.'

As a rule he did not choose to be seen pleasuring with a native – it undermined his authority – but this was a special occasion.

They moved briskly through the village, Barnabas driving to show the paces of the horse, and presently turned to the woods or to what remained of them; there was a tolerable road, made by the timber fellers, which wound uphill towards a grove. The scene was uninteresting, and pervaded by a whitish light that seemed to penetrate every recess. They spoke of local affairs.

'How much of the timber is earmarked for the mines?' inquired Mr Pinmay, in the course of the conversation.

'An increasing amount as the galleries extend deeper into the mountain. I am told that the heat down there is now so great that the miners work unclad. Are they to be fined for this?'

'No. It is impossible to be strict about mines. They constitute a special case.'

'I understand. I am also told that disease among them increases.'

'It does, but then so do our hospitals.'

'I do not understand.'

'Can't you grasp, Barnabas, that under God's permission certain evils attend civilisation, but that if men do God's will the remedies for the evils keep pace? Five years ago you had not a single hospital in this valley.'

'Nor any disease. I understand. Then all my people were strong.'

'There was abundant disease,' corrected the missionary. 'Vice and superstition, to mention no others. And inter-tribal war. Could you have married a lady from another valley five years ago?'

'No. Even as a concubine she would have disgraced me.'

'All concubines are a disgrace.'

'I understand. In regard to this marriage, sir, there is, however, a promise that you made me once.'

'About the mining concession, of course? Exactly. Yes, I never thought you were treated fairly there. I will certainly approach my future brother-in-law to get you some compensation. But you ought to have been more careful at the time. You signed your rights away without consulting me. I am always willing to be consulted.'

'It is not the mining concession,' said Barnabas patiently; although a good steward for the Church, he had grown careless where his own affairs were concerned. 'It is quite another promise.' He seemed to be choosing his words. Speaking slowly and without any appearance of emotion, he said at last: 'Come to Christ.'

'Come to Him indeed,' said Mr Pinmay in slightly reproving tones, for he was not accustomed to receive such an invitation from a spiritual inferior.

Barnabas paused again, then said, 'In the hut.'

'What hut?' He had forgotten.

'The hut with the Mercy Seat.'

Shocked and angry, he exclaimed: 'Barnabas, Barnabas, this is disgraceful. I forbad you ever to mention this subject.'

At that moment the horse drew up at the entrance of the grove. Civilisation tapped and clinked behind them, under a garish sun. The road ended, and a path where two could walk abreast continued into the delicate grey and purple recesses of the trees. Tepid, impersonal, as if he still discussed public affairs, the young man said, 'Let us both be entirely reasonable, sir. God continues to order me to love you. It is my life, whatever else I seem to do. My body and the breath in it are still yours, though you wither them up with this waiting. Come into the last forest, before it is cut down, and I will be kind, and all may end well. But it is now five years since you first said Not yet.'

'It is, and now I say Never.'

'This time you say Never?'

'I do.'

Without replying, Barnabas handed him the reins, and then jerked himself out of the cart. It was a most uncanny movement, which seemed to proceed direct from the will. He scarcely used his hands or rose to his feet before jumping. But his soul uncoiled like a spring, and thrust the cart violently away from it against the ground. Mr Pinmay had heard of such contortions, but never witnessed them; they were startling, they were disgusting. And the descent was equally sinister. Barnabas lay helpless as if the evil uprush had suddenly failed. 'Are you ill?' asked the clergyman.

'No.'

'Then what ails you?'

'No.'

'Do you repent of your words?'

'No.'

'Then you must be punished. As the head of the community you are bound to set an example. You are fined one hundred pounds for backsliding.'

'No.' Then, as if to himself, he said, 'First the grapes of my body are pressed. Then I am silenced. Now I am punished. Night, evening and a day. What remains?'

What should remain? The remark was meaningless. Mr Pinmay drove back alone, rather thoughtful. He would certainly have to return the horse and cart – they had been intended as a bribe – and the hundred pounds must be collected by one of his subordinates. He wished that the whole unsavoury business had not been raked up into the light just before his wedding. Its senselessness alarmed him.

Morning

The concluding five years of Mr Pinmay's ministry were less satisfactory than their predecessors. His marriage was happy, his difficulties few, nothing tangible opposed him, but he was haunted by the scene outside the grove. Could it signify that he himself had not been pardoned? Did God, in His mystery, demand from him that he should cleanse his brother's soul before his own could be accepted? The dark erotic perversion that the chief mistook for Christianity – who had implanted it? He had put this question from him in the press of his earlier dangers, but it intruded itself now that he was safe. Day after day he heard the cold voice of the somewhat scraggy and unattractive native inviting him to sin, or saw the leap from the cart that suggested a dislocated soul. He turned to the Christianity of the valley, but he found no consolation there. He had implanted that too: not in sin, but in reaction against sin, and so its fruits were as bitter. If Barnabas distorted Christ, the valley ignored Him. It was hard, it lacked personality and beauty and emotion and all that Paul Pinmay had admired in his youth. It could produce catechists and organisers, but never a saint. What was the cause of the failure? The hut, the hut. In the concluding years of his stay, he ordered it to be pulled down.

He seldom met Barnabas now. There was no necessity for it, since the chief's usefulness decreased as the community developed and new men pushed their way to the top. Though still helpful when applied to, he lost all capacity for initiative. He moved from his old stockaded enclosure with its memories of independence, and occupied a lofty but small modern house at the top of the village, suitable to his straitened circumstances. Here he and his wife and their children (one more every eleven months) lived in the semi-European style. Sometimes he worked in the garden, although menial labour was regarded as degrading, and he was assiduous at prayer meetings, where he frequented the back row. The missionaries called him a true Christian when they called him anything, and congratulated themselves that witchcraft had no rallying point; he had served their purpose, he began to pass from their talk. Only Mr Pinmay watched him furtively and wondered where his old energies had gone. He would have preferred an outburst to this corrupt acquiescence; he knew now that he could deal with outbursts. He even felt weaker himself, as if the same curse infected them both, and this though he had again and again confessed his own share of the sin to God, and had acquired a natural loathing for it in consequence of his marriage.

He could not really feel much sorrow when he learned that the unfortunate fellow was dying.

Consumption was the cause. One of the imported workers had started an epidemic, and Mr and Mrs Pinmay were busied up to the moment of their own departure, negotiating an extension to the cemetery. They expected to leave the valley before Barnabas did, but during the last week he made, so to speak, a spurt, as if he would outstrip them. His was a very rapid case. He put up no fight. His heart seemed broken. They had little time to devote to individuals, so wide was the scope of their work, still they hurried over to see him one morning, hearing that he had had a fresh haemorrhage, and was not likely to survive the day. 'Poor fellow, poor lad, he was an important factor ten years back – times change,' murmured Mr Pinmay as he pushed the Holy Communion under the seat of the dog cart – Barnabas's own cart, as it happened, for Mrs Pinmay, knowing nothing of the incident, had acquired it cheaply at a sale a couple of years back. As he drove it briskly up through the village Mr Pinmay's heart grew lighter, and he thanked God for permitting Barnabas, since die we must, to pass away at this particular moment; he would not have liked to leave him behind, festering, equivocal, and perhaps acquiring some sinister power.

When they arrived, Mrs Barnabas told them that her husband was still alive, and, she thought, conscious, but in such darkness of spirit that he would not open his eyes or speak. He had been carried up on to the roof, on account of the heat in his room, and his gestures had indicated that he would be left alone. 'But he must not be left alone,' said Mr Pinmay. 'We must watch with him through this dark hour. I will prepare him in the first place.' He climbed the staircase that led through a trapdoor on to the roof. In the shadow of the parapet lay the dying man, coughing gently, and stark naked.

'Vithobai!' he cried in amazement.

He opened his eyes and said, 'Who calls me?'

'You must have some covering, Barnabas,' said Mr Pinmay fussily. He looked round, but there was nothing on the roof except a curious skein of blue flowers threaded round a knife. He took them up. But the other said, 'Do not lay those upon me yet,' and he refrained, remembering that blue is the colour of despair in that valley, just as red is the colour of love. 'I'll get you a shawl,' he continued. 'Why, you are not lying upon a mattress, even.'

'It is my own roof. Or I thought it was until now. My wife and household respected my wishes. They laid me here because it is not the custom of my ancestors to die in a bed.'

'Mrs Barnabas should have known better. You cannot possibly lie on hard asphalt.'

'I have found that I can.'

'Vithobai, Vithobai,' he cried, more upset than he expected. 'Who calls me?'

'You are not going back to your old false gods?'

'Oh no. So near to the end of my life, why should I make any change? These flowers are only a custom, and they comfort me.'

'There is only one comforter...' He glanced around the roof, then fell on his knees. He could save a soul without danger to himself at last. 'Come to Christ,' he said, 'but not in the way that you suppose. The time has come for me to explain. You and I once sinned together, yes, you and your missionary whom you so reverence. You and I must now repent together, yes, such is God's law.' And confusedly, and with many changes of emotion and shiftings of his point of view and reservations, he explained the nature of what had happened ten years ago and its present consequences.

The other made a painful effort to follow, but his eyes kept closing. 'What is all this talk?' he said at last. 'And why do you wait until I am ill and you old?'

'I waited until I could forgive you and ask your forgiveness. It is the hour of your atonement and mine. Put away all despair, forget those wicked flowers. Let us repent and leave the rest to God.'

'I repent, I do not repent...' he wailed.

'Hush! Think what you say.'

'I forgive you, I do not forgive, both are the same. I am good I am evil I am pure I am foul, I am this or that, I am Barnabas, I am Vithobai. What difference does it make now? It is my deeds that await me, and I have no strength left to add to them. No strength, no time. I lie here empty but you fill me up with thoughts, and then press me to speak them that you may have words to remember afterwards, But it is deeds, deeds that count, O my lost brother. Mine are this little house instead of my old great one, this valley which other men own, this cough that kills me, those bastards that continue my race; and that deed in the hut, which you say caused all, and which now you call joy, now sin. How can I remember which it was after all

39

these years, and what difference if I could? It was a deed, it has gone before with the others to be judged.'

'Vithobai,' he pleaded, distressed because he had been called old.

'Who calls me the third time?'

'Kiss me.'

'My mouth is down here.'

'Kiss my forehead – no more – as a sign that I am forgiven. Do not misunderstand me this time... in perfect purity... the holy salutation of Christ. And then say with me: Our Father which art in Heaven, hallowed be Thy name...'

'My mouth is down here,' he repeated wearily.

Mr Pinmay feared to venture the kiss lest Satan took an advantage. He longed to do something human before he had the sinking man carried down to receive the Holy Communion, but he had forgotten how. 'You have forgiven me, my poor fellow,' he worried on. 'If you do not, how can I continue my vocation, or hope for the forgiveness of God?'

The lips moved.

'If you forgive me, move your lips once more, as a sign.'

He became rigid, he was dying.

'You do still love me?'

'My breast is down here.'

'In Christ, I mean.' And uncertain of what he ought to do he laid his head hesitatingly upon the poor skeleton. Vithobai shivered, then looked at him with surprise, pity, affection, disdain, with all, but with little of any, for his Spirit had mainly departed, and only the ghosts of its activities remained. He was a little pleased. He raised a hand painfully, and stroked the scanty hair, golden no longer. He whispered, 'Too late,' but he smiled a little.

'It is never too late,' said Mr Pinmay, permitting a slow encircling movement of the body, the last it would ever accomplish.

'God's mercy is infinite, and endureth for ever and ever. He will give us other opportunities. We have erred in this life but it will not be so in the life to come.'

The dying man seemed to find comfort at last. 'The life to come,' he whispered, but more distinctly. 'I had forgotten it. You are sure it is coming?'

'Even your old false religion was sure of that.'

'And we shall meet in it, you and I?' he asked, with a tender yet reverent caress.

'Assuredly, if we keep God's commandments.'

'Shall we know one another again?'

'Yes, with all spiritual knowledge.'

'And will there be love?'

'In the real and true sense, there will.'

'Real and true love! Ah, that would be joyful.' His voice gained strength, his eyes had an austere beauty as he embraced his friend, parted from him so long by the accidents of earth. Soon God would wipe away all tears. 'The life to come,' he shouted. 'Life, life, eternal life. Wait for me in it.' And he stabbed the missionary through the heart.

The jerk the knife gave brought his own fate hurrying upon him. He had scarcely the strength to push the body to the asphalt or to spread the skein of blue flowers. But he survived for a moment longer, and it was the most exquisite he had ever known. For love was conquered at last and he was again a king, he had sent a messenger before him to announce his arrival in the life to come, as a great chief should. 'I served you for ten years,' he thought, 'and your yoke was hard, but mine will be harder and you shall serve me now for ever and ever.' He dragged himself up, he looked over the parapet. Below him were a horse and cart, beyond, the valley which he had once ruled, the site of the hut, the ruins of his old stockade, the schools, the hospital, the cemetery, the stacks of timber, the polluted stream, all that he had been used to regard as signs of his disgrace. But they signified nothing this morning, they were flying like mist and beneath them, solid and eternal, stretched the kingdom of the dead. He rejoiced as in boyhood, he was expected there now. Mounting on the corpse, he climbed higher, raised his arms over his head, sunlit, naked, victorious, leaving all disease and humiliation behind him, and he swooped like a falcon from the parapet in pursuit of the terrified shade.

Dr Woolacott

For this, from stiller seats we came
— CYMBELINE, V. iv

People, several of them, crossing the park...

Clesant said to himself, 'There is no reason I should not live for years now that I have given up the violin,' and leant back with the knowledge that he had faced a fact. From where he lay, he could see a little of the garden and a little of the park, a little of the fields and the river, and hear a little of the tennis; a little of everything was what was good for him, and what Dr Woolacott had prescribed. Every few weeks he must expect a relapse, and he would never be able to travel or marry or manage the estates, still there, he didn't want to much, he didn't much want to do anything. An electric bell connected him with the house, the strong beautiful slightly alarming house where his father had died, still there, not so very alarming, not so bad lying out in the tepid sun and watching the colourless shapeless country people...

No, there was no reason he should not live for years.

'In 1990, why even 2000 is possible, I am young,' he thought. Then he frowned for Dr Woolacott was bound to be dead by 2000, and the treatment might not be continued intelligently. The anxiety made his head ache, the trees and grass turned black or crimson, and he nearly rang his bell. Soothed by the advancing figures, he desisted. Looking for mushrooms apparently, they soothed him because of their inadequacy. No mushrooms grew in the park. He felt friendly and called out in his gentle voice, 'Come here.'

'Oh aye,' came the answer.

'I'm the squire, I want you a moment, it's all right.'

Set in motion, the answerer climbed over the park fence. Clesant had not intended him to do this, and fearful of being bored said, 'You'll find no mushrooms here, but they'll give you a drink or anything else you fancy up at the house.'

'Sir, the squire, did you say?'

'Yes; I pass for the squire.'

'The one who's sick?'

'Yes, that one.'

'I'm sorry.'

'Thank you, thanks,' said the boy, pleased by the unexpected scrap of sympathy.

'Sir…'

'All right, what is it?' he smiled encouragingly.

'Sick of what illness?'

Clesant hesitated. As a rule he resented that question, but this morning it pleased him, it was as if he too had been detected by friendly eyes zigzagging in search of a treasure which did not exist. He replied, 'Of being myself perhaps! Well, what they call functional. Nothing organic. I can't die, but my heart makes my nerves go wrong, my nerves my digestion, then my head aches, so I can't sleep, which affects my heart, and round we go again. However, I'm better this morning.'

'When shall you be well?'

He gave the contemptuous laugh of the chronic invalid. 'Well. That's a very different question. It depends. It depends on a good many things. On how carefully I live. I must avoid all excitement, I must never get tired, I mustn't be – ' He was going to say 'mustn't be intimate with people', but it was no use employing expressions which would be meaningless to a farm worker, and such the man appeared to be, so he changed it to 'I must do as Dr Woolacott tells me.'

'Oh, Woolacott…'

'Of course you know him, everyone round here does, marvellous doctor.'

'Yes I know Woolacott.'

Clesant looked up, intrigued by something positive in the tone of the voice.

'Woolacott, Woolacott, so I must be getting on.' Not quite as he had come, he vaulted over the park palings, paused, repeated 'Woolacott' and walked rapidly after his companions, who had almost disappeared.

A servant now answered the bell. It had failed to ring the first time, which would have been annoying had the visitor proved tedious. The little incident was over now, and nothing else disturbed the peace of the morning. The park, the garden, the sounds from the tennis, all reassumed their due proportions, but it seemed to Clesant that they were pleasanter and more significant than they had been, that the colours of the grass and the shapes of the trees had beauty, that the sun wandered with a purpose through the sky, that the little clouds, wafted by westerly airs, were moving against the course of doom and fate, and were inviting him to follow them.

2

Continuance of convalescence… tea in the gunroom. The gunroom, a grand place in the old squire's time, much energy had flowed through it intellectual and bodily. Now the bookcases were locked, the trophies between them desolate, the tall shallow cupboard designed for fishing rods and concealed in the wainscoting contained only medicine bottles and air cushions. Still it was Clesant's nearest approach to normality, for the rest of his household had tea in the gunroom too. There was innocuous talk as they flitted out and in, pursuing their affairs like birds, and troubling him only with the external glint of their plumage. He knew nothing about them, although they were his guardians and familiars; even their sex left no impression on his mind. Throned on the pedestal of a sofa he heard them speak of their wishes and plans, and give one another to understand that they had passionate impulses, while he barricaded himself in the circle of his thoughts.

He was thinking about music.

Was it quite out of the question that he should take up the violin again? He felt better, the morning in the garden had started him upon a good road, a refreshing sleep had followed. Now a languorous yearning filled him, which might not the violin satisfy? The effect might be the contrary, the yearning might turn to pain, yet even pain seemed unlikely in this kindly house, this house which had not always been kindly, yet surely this afternoon it was accepting him.

A stranger entered his consciousness – a young man in good if somewhat provincial clothes, with a pleasant and resolute expression upon his face. People always were coming into the house on some business or other, and then going out of it. He stopped in the middle of the room, evidently a little shy. No one spoke to him for the reason that no one remained: they had all gone away while Clesant followed his meditations. Obliged to exert himself for a moment, Clesant said, 'I'm sorry – I expect you're wanting one of the others.'

He smiled and twiddled his cap.

'I'm afraid I mustn't entertain you myself. I'm something of an invalid, and this is my first day up. I suffer from one of those wretched functional troubles – fortunately nothing organic.'

Smiling more broadly, he remarked: 'Oh aye.'

Clesant clutched at his heart, jumped up, sat down, burst out laughing. It was that farmworker who had been crossing the park.

'Thought I'd surprise you, thought I'd give you a turn,' he cried gaily. 'I've come for that drink you promised.'

Clesant couldn't speak for laughing, the whole room seemed to join in, it was a tremendous joke.

'I was around in my working kit when you invited me this morning, so I thought after I'd washed myself up a bit and had a shave my proper course was to call and explain,' he continued more seriously. There was something fresh and rough in his voice which caught at the boy's heart.

'But who on earth are you, who are you working for?'

'For you.'

'Oh nonsense, don't be silly.'

''Tisn't nonsense, I'm not silly, I'm one of your farm-hands. Rather an unusual one, if you like. Still, I've been working here for the last three months, ask your bailiff if I haven't. But I say – I've kept thinking about you – how are you?'

'Better – because I saw you this morning!'

'That's fine. Now you've seen me this afternoon you'll be well.'

But this last remark was flippant, and the visitor through making it lost more than the ground he had gained. It reminded Clesant that he had been guilty of laughter and of rapid movement, and he replied in reproving tones, 'To be well and to be better are very different. I'm afraid one can't get well from one's self. Excuse me if we don't talk any more. It's so bad for my heart.' He closed his eyes. He opened them again immediately. He had had, during that instant of twilight, a curious and pleasurable sensation. However, there was the young man still over at the farther side of the room. He was smiling. He was attractive – fresh as a daisy, strong as a horse. His shyness had gone.

'Thanks for that tea, a treat,' he said, lighting a cigarette. 'Now for who I am. I'm a farmer – or rather, going to be a farmer. I'm only an agricultural labourer now – exactly what you took me for this morning. I wasn't dressing up or posing with that broad talk. It's come natural to say "Oh aye", especially when startled.'

'Did I startle you?'

'Yes, you weren't in my mind.'

'I thought you were looking for mushrooms.'

'So I was. We all do when we're shifting across, and when there's a market we sell them. I've been living with that sort all the summer, your regular hands, temporaries like myself, tramps, sharing their work, thinking their thoughts when they have any.' He paused. 'I like them.'

'Do they like you?'

'Oh well...' He laughed, drew a ring off his finger, laid it on the palm of his hand, looked at it for a moment, put it on again. All his gestures were definite and a trifle unusual. 'I've no pride anyway, nor any reason to have. I only have my health, and I didn't always have that. I've known what it is to be an invalid, though no one guesses it now.' He looked across gently at Clesant. He seemed to say, 'Come to me, and you shall be as happy as I am and as strong.' He gave a short account of his life. He dealt in facts, very much so when they arrived – and the tale he unfolded was high-spirited and a trifle romantic here and there, but in no way remarkable. Aged twenty-two, he was the son of an engineer at Wolverhampton, his two brothers were also engineers, but he himself had always taken after his mother's family, and preferred country life. All his holidays on a farm. The war. After which he took up agriculture seriously, and went through a course at Cirencester. The course terminated last spring, he had done well, his people were about to invest money in him, but he himself felt 'too scientific' after it all. He was determined to 'get down into the manure' and feel people instead of thinking about them. 'Later on it's too late.' So off he went and roughed it, with a few decent clothes in a suitcase, and now and then, just for the fun of the thing, he took them out and dressed up. He described the estate, how decent the bailiff was, how sorry people seemed to be about the squire's illness, how he himself got a certain amount of time off, practically any evening. Extinguishing his cigarette, he put back what was left of it into his case for future use, laid a hand upon either knee, smiled.

There was a silence. Clesant could not think of anything to say, and began to tremble.

'Oh, my name – '

'Oh yes, of course, what's your name?'

'Let me write it down, my address too. Both my Wolver-hampton address I'll give you, also where I'm lodging here, so if ever – got a pencil?'

'Yes.'

'Don't get up.'

He came over and sat on the sofa; his weight sent a tremor, the warmth and sweetness of his body began casting nets.

'And now we've no paper.'

'Never mind,' said Clesant, his heart beating violently.

'Talking's better, isn't it?'

'Yes.'

'Or even not talking.' His hand came nearer, his eyes danced round the room, which began to fill with a golden haze. He beckoned, and Clesant moved into his arms. Clesant had often been proud of his disease but never, never of his body, it had never occurred to him that he could provoke desire. The sudden revelation shattered him, he fell from his pedestal, but not alone, there was someone to cling to, broad shoulders, a sun-burnt throat, lips that parted as they touched him to murmur – 'And to hell with Woolacott.'

Woolacott! He had completely forgotten the doctor's exist-ence. Woolacott! The word crashed between them and exploded with a sober light, and he saw in the light of the years that had passed and would come how ridiculously he was behaving. To hell with Woolacott, indeed! What an idea! His charming new friend must be mad. He started, recoiled, and exclaimed, 'Whatever made you say that?'

The other did not reply. He looked rather foolish, and he too recoiled, and leant back in the opposite corner of the sofa, wiping his forehead. At last he said, 'He's not a good doctor.'

'Why, he's our family doctor, he's everyone's doctor round here!'

'I didn't mean to be rude – it slipped out. I just had to say it, it must have sounded curious.'

'Oh, all right then,' said the boy, willing enough to be mollified. But the radiance had passed and no effort of theirs could recall it.

The young man took out his unfinished cigarette, and raised it towards his lips. He was evidently a good deal worried. 'Perhaps I'd better explain what I meant,' he said.

'As you like, it doesn't matter.'

'Got a match?'

'I'm afraid I haven't.'

He went for one to the farther side of the room, and sat down there again. Then he began: 'I'm perfectly straight – I'm not trying to work in some friend of my own as your doctor. I only can't bear to think of this particular one coming to your house – this grand house – you so rich and important at the first sight and yet so awfully undefended and deceived.' His voice faltered. 'No, we won't talk it over. You're right. We've found each other, nothing else matters, it's a chance in a million we've found each other. I'd do anything for you, I'd die if I could for you, and there's this one thing you must do straight away for me: sack Woolacott.'

'Tell me what you've got against him instead of talking sentimentally.'

He hardened at once. 'Sentimental, was I? All right, what I've got against Woolacott is that he never makes anyone well, which seems a defect in a doctor. I may be wrong.'

'Yes, you're wrong,' said Clesant; the mere repetition of the doctor's name was steadying him. 'I've been under him for years.'

'So I should think.'

'Of course, I'm different, I'm not well, it's not natural for me to be well, I'm not a fair test, but other people – '

'Which other people?'

The names of Dr Woolacott's successful cases escaped him for the moment. They filled the centre of his mind, yet the moment he looked at them they disappeared.

'Quite so,' said the other. 'Woolacott,' he kept on saying. 'Woolacott! I've my eye on him. What's life after twenty-five? Impotent, blind, paralytic. What's life before it unless you're fit? Woolacott! Even the poor can't escape. The crying, the limping, the nagging, the medicine bottles, the running sores – in the cottages too; kind Dr Woolacott won't let them stop… You think I'm mad, but it's not your own thought you're thinking: Woolacott stuck it ready diseased into your mind.'

Clesant sighed. He looked at the arms now folded hard against each other, and longed to feel them around him. He had only to say, 'Very well, I'll change doctors,' and immediately… But he never hesitated. Life until 1990 or 2000 retained the prior claim. 'He keeps people alive,' he persisted.

'Alive for what?'

'And there's always the marvellously unselfish work he did during the war.'

'Did he not. I saw him doing it.'

'Oh – it was in France you knew him?'

'Was it not. He was at his marvellously unselfish work night and day, and not a single man he touched ever got well.

Woolacott dosed, Woolacott inoculated, Woolacott operated, Woolacott spoke a kind word even, and there they were and here they are.'

'Were you in hospital yourself?'

'Oh aye, a shell. This hand – ring and all mashed and twisted, the head – hair's thick enough on it now, but brain stuck out then, so did my guts, I was a butcher's shop. A perfect case for Woolacott. Up he came with his "Let me patch you up, do let me just patch you up", oh, patience itself and all that, but I took his measure, I was only a boy then, but I refused.'

'Can one refuse in a military hospital?'

'You can refuse anywhere.'

'I hadn't realised you'd been wounded. Are you all right now?'

'Yes, thanks,' and he resumed his grievances. The pleasant purple-grey suit, the big well-made shoes and soft white collar all suggested a sensible country lad on his holiday, perhaps on courtship – farmhand or farmer, countrified anyway. Yet with them went this wretched war-obsession, this desire to be revenged on a man who had never wronged him and must have forgotten his existence. 'He is stronger than I am,' he said angrily. 'He can fight alone, I can't. My great disadvantage – never could fight alone. I counted on you to help, but you prefer to let me down, you pretended at first you'd join up with me – you're no good.'

'Look here, you'll have to be going. So much talk is fatal for me, I simply mustn't get overtired. I've already far exceeded my allowance, and anyhow I can't enter into this sort of thing. Can you find your own way out, or shall I ring this bell?' For inserted into the fabric of the sofa was an electric bell.

'I'll go. I know where I'm not wanted. Don't you worry, you'll never see me again.' And he slapped his cap on to his head and swung to the door. The normal life of the house entered the gunroom as he opened it – servants, inmates, talking in the passages, in the hall outside. It disconcerted him, he came back with a complete change of manner, and before ever he spoke Clesant had the sense of an incredible catastrophe moving up towards them both.

'Is there another way out?' he inquired anxiously.

'No, of course not. Go out the way you came in.'

'I didn't tell you, but the fact is I'm in trouble.'

'How dare you, I mustn't be upset, this is the kind of thing that makes me ill,' he wailed.

'I can't meet those people – they've heard of something I did out in France.'

'What was it?'

'I can't tell you.'

In the sinister silence, Clesant's heart resumed its violent beating, and though the door was now closed voices could be heard through it. They were coming. The stranger rushed at the window and tried to climb out. He plunged about, soiling his freshness, and whimpering, 'Hide me.'

'There's nowhere.'

'There must be…'

'Only that cupboard,' said Clesant in a voice not his own.

'I can't find it,' he gasped, thumping stupidly on the panelling. 'Do it for me. Open it. They're coming.'

Clesant dragged himself up and across the floor, he opened the cupboard, and the man bundled in and hid, and that was how it ended.

Yes, that's how it ends, that's what comes of being kind to handsome strangers and wanting to touch them. Aware of all his weaknesses, Dr Woolacott had warned him against this one. He crawled back to the sofa, where a pain stabbed him through the heart and another struck between the eyes. He was going to be ill.

The voices came nearer, and with the cunning of a sufferer he decided what he must do. He must betray his late friend and pretend to have trapped him on purpose in the cupboard, cry 'Open it...'

The voices entered. They spoke of the sounds of a violin. A violin had apparently been heard playing in the great house for the last half-hour, and no one could find out where it was. Playing all sorts of music, gay, grave and passionate. But never completing a theme. Always breaking off. A beautiful instrument. Yet so unsatisfying... leaving the hearers much sadder than if it had never performed. What was the use (someone asked) of music like that? Better silence absolute than this aimless disturbance of our peace. The discussion broke off, his distress had been observed, and like a familiar refrain rose up 'Telephone, nurse, doctor...' Yes, it was coming again – the illness, merely functional, the heart had affected the nerves, the muscles, the brain. He groaned, shrieked, but love died last; as he writhed in convulsions he cried: 'Don't go to the cupboard, no one's there.'

So they went to it. And no one was there. It was as it had always been since his father's death – shallow, tidy, a few medicine bottles on the upper shelf, a few cushions stored on the lower.

3

Collapse... He fell back into the apparatus of decay without further disaster, and in a few hours any other machinery for life became unreal. It always was like this, increasingly like this, when he was ill. Discomfort and pain brought their compensation, because they were so superbly organised. His bedroom, the anteroom where the night nurse sat, the bathroom and the tiny kitchen, throbbed like a nerve in the corner of the great house, and elsewhere normal life proceeded, people pursued their avocations in channels which did not disturb him.

Delirium… The nurse kept coming in, she performed medical incantations and took notes against the doctor's arrival. She did not make him better, he grew worse, but disease knows its harmonies as well as health, and through its soft advances now ran the promise, 'You shall live to grow old.'

'I did something wrong, tell me, what was it?' It made him happy to abase himself before his disease, nor was this colloquy their first.

'Intimacy,' the disease replied.

'I remember… Do not punish me this once, let me live and I will be careful. Oh, save me from him.'

'No – from yourself. Not from him. He does not exist. He is an illusion, whom you created in the garden because you wanted to feel you were attractive.'

'I know I am not attractive, I will never excite myself again, but he does exist, I think.'

'No.'

'He may be death, but he does exist.'

'No. He never came into the gunroom. You only wished that he would. He never sat down on the sofa by your side and made love. You handed a pencil, but he never took it, you fell into his arms, but they were not there, it has all been a daydream of the kind forbidden. And when the others came in and opened the cupboard: your muscular and intelligent farmhand, your saviour from Wolverhampton in his Sunday suit – was he there?'

'No, he was not,' the boy sobbed.

'No, he was not,' came an echo, 'but perhaps I am here.'

The disease began to crouch and gurgle. There was the sound of a struggle, a spewing sound, a fall. Clesant, not greatly frightened, sat up and peered into the chaos. The nightmare passed, he felt better. Something survived from it, an echo that said 'Here,

here.' And, he not dissenting, bare feet seemed to walk to the little table by his side, and hollow, filled with the dark, a shell of nakedness bent towards him and sighed 'Here.'

Clesant declined to reply.

'Here is the end, unless you...' Then silence. Then, as if emitted by a machine, the syllables 'Oh aye.'

Clesant, after thought, put out his hand and touched the bell.

'I put her to sleep as I passed her, this is my hour, I can do that much...' He seemed to gather strength from any recognition of his presence, and to say, 'Tell my story for me, explain how I got here, pour life into me and I shall live as before when our bodies touched.' He sighed. 'Come home with me now, perhaps it is a farm. I have just enough power. Come away with me for an evening to my earthly lodging, easily managed by a... the... such a visit would be love. Ah, that was the word – love – why they pursued me and still know I am in the house; love was the word they cannot endure, I have remembered it at last.'

Then Clesant spoke, sighing in his turn. 'I don't even know what is real, so how can I know what is love? Unless it is excitement, and of that I am afraid. Do not love me, whatever you are; at all events this is my life and no one shall disturb it; a little sleep followed by a little pain.'

And his speech evoked strength. More powerfully the other answered now, giving instances and arguments, throwing into sentences the glow they had borne during daylight. Clesant was drawn into a struggle, but whether to reach or elude the hovering presence he did not know. There was always a barrier either way, always his own nature. He began calling for people to come, and the adversary, waxing lovely and powerful, struck them dead before they could waken and help. His household perished, the whole earth was thinning, one instant more and he would be alone with his ghost – and then through the walls of the house he saw the lights of a car rushing across the park.

It was Dr Woolacott at last.

Instantly the spell broke, the dead revived, and went downstairs to receive life's universal lord; and he – he was left with a human being who had somehow trespassed and been caught, and blundered over the furniture in the dark, bruising his defenceless body, and whispering 'Hide me.'

And Clesant took pity on him again, and lifted the clothes of the bed, and they hid.

Voices approached, a great company, Dr Woolacott leading his army. They touched, their limbs intertwined, they gripped and grew mad with delight, yet through it all sounded the tramp of that army.

'They are coming.'

'They will part us.'

'Clesant, shall I take you away from all this?'

'Have you still the power?'

'Yes, until Woolacott sees me.'

'Oh, what is your name?'

'I have none.'

'Where is your home?'

'Woolacott calls it the grave.'

'Shall I be with you in it?'

'I can promise you that. We shall be together for ever and ever, we shall never be ill, and never grow old.'

'Take me.'

They entwined more closely, their lips touched never to part, and then something gashed him where life had concentrated, and Dr Woolacott, arriving too late, found him dead on the floor.

The doctor examined the room carefully. It presented its usual appearance, yet it reminded him of another place. Dimly, from France, came the vision of a hospital ward, dimly the sound of his own voice saying to a mutilated recruit, 'Do let me patch you up, oh but you must just let me patch you up...'

Arthur Snatchfold

I

Conway (Sir Richard Conway) woke early, and went to the window to have a look at the Trevor Donaldsons' garden. Too green. A flight of mossy steps led up from the drive to a turfed amphitheatre. This contained a number of trees of the lead-pencil persuasion, and a number of flower beds, profuse with herbaceous promises which would certainly not be fulfilled that weekend. The summer was heavy-leaved and at a moment between flowerings, and the gardener, though evidently expensive, had been caught bending. Bounding the amphitheatre was a high yew hedge, an imposing background had there been any foreground, and behind the hedge a heavy wood shut the sky out. Of course what was wanted was colour. Delphinium, salvia, red-hot poker, zinnias, tobacco plant, anything. Leaning out of the baronial casement, Conway considered this, while he waited for his tea. He was not an artist, nor a philosopher, but he liked exercising his mind when he had nothing else to do, as on this Sunday morning, this country morning, with so much ahead to be eaten, and so little to be said.

The visit, like the view, threatened monotony. Dinner had been dull. His own spruce grey head, gleaming in the mirrors, really seemed the brightest object about. Trevor Donaldson's head was mangy, Mrs Donaldson's combed up into bastions of iron. He did not get unduly fussed at the prospect of boredom. He was a man of experience with plenty of resources and plenty of armour, and he was a decent human being too. The Donaldsons were his inferiors – they had not travelled or read or gone in for sport or love, they were merely his business allies, linked to him by a common interest in aluminium. Still, he must try to make things nice, since they had been so good as to invite him down. 'But it's not so easy to make things nice for us business people,' he reflected, as he listened to the chonk of a blackbird, the clink of a milk can, and the distant self-communings of an electric pump. 'We're not stupid or uncultivated, we can use our minds when required, we can go to concerts when we're not too tired, we've invested – even Trevor Donaldson has – in the sense of humour. But I'm afraid we don't get much pleasure out of it all. No. Pleasure's been left out of our packet.' Business occupied him increasingly since his wife's death. He brought an active mind to bear on it, and was quickly becoming rich.

He looked at the dull costly garden. It improved. A man had come into it from the back of the yew hedge. He had on a canary-coloured shirt, and the effect was exactly right. The whole scene blazed. That was what the place wanted – not a flowerbed, but a man, who advanced with a confident tread down the amphitheatre, and as he came nearer Conway saw that besides being proper to the colour scheme he was a very proper youth. His shoulders were broad, his face sensuous and open, his eyes, screwed up against the light, promised good temper. One arm shot out at an angle, the other supported a milk can. 'Good morning, nice morning,' he called, and he sounded happy.

'Good morning, nice morning,' he called back. The man continued at a steady pace, turned left and disappeared in the direction of the servants' entrance, where an outburst of laughter welcomed him.

Conway hoped he might return by the same route, and waited. 'That is a nice-looking fellow, I do like the way he holds himself, and probably no nonsense about him,' he thought. But the vision had departed, the sunlight stopped, the garden turned stodgy and green again, and the maid came in with his tea. She said, 'I'm sorry to be late, we were waiting for the milk, sir.' The man had not called him sir, and the omission flattered him. 'Good morning, sir' would have been the more natural saluta-tion to an elderly stranger, a wealthy customer's guest. But the vigorous voice had shouted 'Good morning, nice morning,' as if they were equals.

Where had he gone off to now, he and his voice? To finish his round, welcomed at house after house, and then for a bathe perhaps, his shirt golden on the grass beside him. Ruddy brown to the waist he would show now… What was his name? Was he a local? Sir Richard put these questions to himself as he dressed, but not vehemently. He was not a sentimentalist, there was no danger of him being shattered for the day. He would have liked to meet the vision again, and spend the whole of Sunday with it, giving it a slap-up lunch at the hotel, hiring a car, which they would drive alternately, treating it to the pictures in the neighbouring town, and returning with it, after one drink too much, through dusky lanes. But that was sheer nonsense, even if the vision had been agreeable to the programme. He was staying with the Trevor Donaldsons; and he must not repay their hospitality by moping. Dressed in a cheerful grey, he ran downstairs to the breakfast room. Mrs Donaldson was already there, and she asked him how his daughters were getting on at their school.

Then his host followed, rubbing his hands together, and saying 'Aha, aha!' and when they had eaten they went into the other garden, the one which sloped towards the water, and started talking business. They had not intended to do this, but there was also of their company a Mr Clifford Clarke, and when Trevor Donaldson, Clifford Clarke and Richard Conway got together it was impossible that aluminium should escape. Their voices deepened, their heads nodded or shook as they recalled vast sums that had been lost through unsound investments or misapplied advice. Conway found himself the most intelligent of the three, the quickest at taking a point, the strongest at following an argument. The moments passed, the blackbird chonk-chonked unheeded, unnoticed was the failure of the gardener to produce anything but tightly furled geraniums, unnoticed the ladies on the lawn, who wanted to get some golf. At last the hostess called, 'Trevor! Is this a holiday or isn't it?' and they stopped, feeling rather ashamed. The cars came round, and soon they were five miles away, on the course, taking their turn in a queue of fellow merrymakers. Conway was good at golf, and got what excitement he could from it, but as soon as the ball flew off he was aware of a slight sinking feeling. This occupied them till lunch. After coffee they walked down to the water, and played with the dogs – Mrs Donaldson bred Sealyhams. Several neighbours came to tea, and now the animation rested with Donaldson, for he fancied himself as a country magnate, and wanted to show how well he was settling into the part. There was a good deal of talk about local conditions, women's institutes, education through discipline, and poaching. Conway found all this quite nonsensical and unreal. People who are not feudal should not play at feudalism, and all magistrates (this he said aloud) ought to be trained and ought to be paid. Since he was well-bred, he said it in a form which did not give offence. Thus the day wore away, and they filled in the interval before dinner by driving to see a ruined monastery. What on earth had they got to do with a monastery? Nothing at all. Nothing at all. He caught sight of Clifford Clarke looking mournfully at a rose window, and he got the feeling that they were all of them looking for something which was not there, that there was an empty chair at the table, a card missing from the bridge-pack, a ball lost in the gorse, a stitch dropped in the shirt; that the chief guest had not come. On their way out they passed through the village, on their way back past a cinema, which was giving a Wild West stunt. They returned through darkling lanes. They did not say, 'Thank you! What a delightful day!' That would be saved up for tomorrow morning, and for the final gratitude of departure. Every word would be needed then. 'I *have* enjoyed myself, I *have*, absolutely marvellous!' the women would chant, and the men would grunt, as if moved beyond words, and the host and hostess would cry, 'Oh but come again, then, come again.' Into the void the little unmemorable visit would fall, like a leaf it would fall upon similar leaves, but Conway wondered whether it hadn't been, so to speak, specially negative, out of the way unflowering, whether a champion, one bare arm at an angle, hadn't carried away to the servants' quarters some refreshment which was badly needed in the smoking room.

'Well, perhaps we shall see, we may yet find out,' he thought, as he went up to bed, carrying with him his raincoat.

For he was not one to give in and grumble. He believed in pleasure; he had a free mind and an active body, and he knew that pleasure cannot be won without courage and coolness. The Donaldsons were all very well, but they were not the whole of his life. His daughters were all very well, but the same held good of them. The female sex was all very well and he was addicted to it, but permitted himself an occasional deviation. He set his alarm watch for an hour slightly earlier than the hour at which he had woken in the morning, and he put it under his pillow, and he fell asleep looking quite young.

Seven o'clock tinkled. He glanced into the passage, then put on his raincoat and thick slippers, and went to the window.

It was a silent sunless morning, and seemed earlier than it actually was. The green of the garden and of the trees was filmed with grey, as if it wanted wiping. Presently the electric pump started. He looked at his watch again, slipped down the stairs, out of the house, across the amphitheatre and through the yew hedge. He did not run, in case he was seen and had to explain. He moved at the maximum pace possible for a gentleman, known to be an original, who fancies an early stroll in his pyjamas. 'I thought I'd have a look at your formal garden, there wouldn't have been time after breakfast' would have been the line. He had of course looked at it the day before, also at the wood. The wood lay before him now, and the sun was just tipping into it. There were two paths through the bracken, a broad and a narrow. He waited until he heard the milk can approaching down the narrow path. Then he moved quickly, and they met, well out of sight of the Donaldsonian demesne.

'Hullo!' he called in his easy out-of-doors voice; he had several voices, and knew by instinct which was wanted.

'Hullo! Somebody's out early!'

'You're early yourself.'

'Me? Whor'd the milk be if I worn't?' the milkman grinned, throwing his head back and coming to a standstill. Seen at close quarters he was coarse, very much of the people and of the thick-fingered earth; a hundred years ago his type was trodden into the mud, now it burst and flowered and didn't care a damn.

'You're the morning delivery, eh?'

'Looks like it.' He evidently proposed to be facetious – the clumsy fun which can be so delightful when it falls from the proper lips. 'I'm not the evening delivery anyway, and I'm not the butcher nor the grocer, nor'm I the coals.'

'Live around here?'

'Maybe. Maybe I don't. Maybe I flop about in them planes.'

'You live around here, I bet.'

'What if I do?'

'If you do you do. And if I don't I don't.'

This fatuous retort was a success, and was greeted with doubled-up laughter. 'If you don't you don't! Ho, you're a funny one! There's a thing to say! If you don't you don't! Walking about in yer night things, too, you'll ketch a cold you will, that'll be the end of you! Stopping back in the 'otel, I suppose?'

'No. Donaldson's. You saw me there yesterday.'

'Oh, Donaldson's, that's it. You was the old granfa' at the upstairs window.'

'Old granfa' indeed… I'll granfa' you,' and he tweaked at the impudent nose. It dodged, it seemed used to this sort of thing. There was probably nothing the lad wouldn't consent to if properly handled, partly out of mischief, partly to oblige. 'Oh, by the way…' and he felt the shirt as if interested in the quality of its material. 'What was I going to say?' and he gave the zip at the throat a downward pull. Much slid into view. 'Oh, I know – when's this round of yours over?'

''Bout eleven. Why?'

'Why not?'

''Bout eleven *at night*. Ha ha. Got yer there. Eleven at night. What you want to arst all them questions for? We're strangers, aren't we?'

'How old are you?'

'Ninety, same as yourself.'

'What's your address?'

'There you go on! Hi! I like that. Arstin questions after I tell you No.'

'Got a girl? Ever heard of a pint? Ever heard of two?'

'Go on. Get out.' But he suffered his forearm to be worked between massaging fingers, and he set down his milk can. He was amused. He was charmed. He was hooked, and a touch would land him.

'You look like a boy who looks all right,' the elder man breathed.

'Oh, *stop* it… All right, I'll go with you.'

Conway was entranced. Thus, exactly thus, should the smaller pleasures of life be approached. They understood one another with a precision impossible for lovers. He laid his face on the warm skin over the clavicle, hands nudged him behind, and presently the sensation for which he had planned so cleverly was over. It was part of the past. It had fallen like a flower upon similar flowers.

He heard 'You all right?' It was over there too, part of a different past. They were lying deeper in the wood, where the fern was highest. He did not reply, for it was pleasant to lie stretched thus and to gaze up through bracken fronds at the distant treetops and the pale blue sky, and feel the exquisite pleasure fade.

'That was what you wanted, wasn't it?' Propped on his elbows, the young man looked down anxiously. All his roughness and pertness had gone, and he only wanted to know whether he had been a success.

'Yes... Lovely.'

'Lovely? You say lovely?' he beamed, prodding gently with his stomach.

'Nice boy, nice shirt, nice everything.'

'That a fact?'

Conway guessed that he was vain, the better sort often are, and laid on the flattery thick to please him, praised his comeliness, his thrusting thrashing strength; there was plenty to praise. He liked to do this and to see the broad face grinning and feel the heavy body on him. There was no cynicism in the flattery, he was genuinely admiring and gratified.

'So you enjoyed that?'

'Who wouldn't?'

'Pity you didn't tell me yesterday.'

'I didn't know how to.'

'I'd a met you down where I have my swim. You could 'elped me strip, you'd like that. Still, we mustn't grumble.' He gave Conway a hand and pulled him up, and brushed and tidied the raincoat like an old friend. 'We could get seven years for this, couldn't we?'

'Not seven years, still we'd get something nasty. Madness, isn't it? What can it matter to anyone else if you and I don't mind?'

'Oh, I suppose they've to occupy themselves with somethink or other,' and he took up the milk can to go on.

'Half a minute, boy – do take this and get yourself some trifle with it.' He produced a note which he had brought on the chance.

'I didn't do it fer that.'

'I know you didn't.'

'Naow, we was each as bad as the other... Naow... keep yer money.'

'I'd be pleased if you would take it. I expect I'm better off than you and it might come in useful. To take out your girl, say, or towards your next new suit. However, please yourself, of course.'

'Can you honestly afford it?'

'Honestly.'

'Well, I'll find a way to spend it, no doubt. People don't always behave as nice as you, you know.'

Conway could have returned the compliment. The affair had been trivial and crude, and yet they both had behaved perfectly. They would never meet again, and they did not exchange names. After a hearty handshake, the young man swung away down the path, the sunlight and the shadow rushing over his back. He did not turn round, but his arm, jerking sideways to balance him, waved an acceptable farewell. The green flowed over his brightness, the path bent, he disappeared. Back he went to his own life, and through the quiet of the morning his laugh could be heard as he whooped at the maids.

Conway waited for a few moments, as arranged, and then he went back too. His luck held. He met no one, either in the amphitheatre garden or on the stairs, and after he had been in his room for a minute the maid arrived with his early tea. 'I'm sorry the milk was late again, sir,' she said. He enjoyed it, bathed and shaved and dressed himself for town. It was the figure of a superior city-man which was reflected in the mirror as he tripped downstairs. The car came round after breakfast to take him to the station, and he was completely sincere when he told the Trevor Donaldsons that he had had an out-of-the-way pleasant weekend. They believed him, and their faces grew brighter. 'Come again then, come by all means again,' they cried as he slid off. In the train he read the papers rather less than usual and smiled to himself rather more. It was so pleasant to have been completely right over a stranger, even down to little details like the texture of the skin. It flattered his vanity. It increased his sense of power.

2

He did not see Trevor Donaldson again for some weeks. Then they met in London at his club, for a business talk and a spot of lunch. Circumstances which they could not control had rendered them less friendly. Owing to regrouping in the financial world, their interests were now opposed, and if one of them stood to make money out of aluminium the other stood to lose. So the talk had been cautious. Donaldson, the weaker man, felt tired and worried after it. He had not, to his knowledge, made a mistake, but he might have slipped unwittingly, and be poorer, and have to give up his county state. He looked at his host with hostility and wished he could harm him. Sir Richard was aware of this, but felt no hostility in return. For one thing, he was going to win, for another, hating never interested him. This was probably the last occasion on which they would foregather socially; but he exercised his usual charm. He wanted, too, to find out during lunch how far Donaldson was aware of his own danger. Clifford Clarke (who was allied with him) had failed to do this.

After adjourning to the cloakroom and washing their hands at adjacent basins, they sat opposite each other at a little table. Down the long room sat other pairs of elderly men, eating, drinking, talking quietly, instructing the waiters. Inquiries were exchanged about Mrs Donaldson and the young Miss Conways, and there were some humorous references to golf. Then Donaldson said, with a change in his voice, 'Golf's all you say, and the great advantage of it in these days is that you get it practically anywhere. I used to think our course was good, for a little country course, but it is far below the average. This is somewhat of a disappointment to us both, since we settled down there specially for the golf. The fact is, the country is not at all what it seems when first you go there.'

'So I've always heard.'

'My wife likes it, of course, she has her Sealyhams, she has her flowers, she has her local charities – though in these days one's not supposed to speak of "charity". I don't know why. I should have thought it was a good word, charity. She runs the Women's Institute, so far as it consents to be run, but Conway, Conway, you'd never believe how offhand the village women are in these days. They don't elect Mrs Donaldson president yearly as a matter of course. She takes turn and turn with cottagers.'

'Oh, that's the spirit of the age, of course. One's always running into it in some form or other. For instance, I don't get nearly the deference I did from my clerks.'

'But better work from them, no doubt,' said Donaldson gloomily.

'No. But probably they're better men.'

'Well, perhaps the ladies at the Women's Institute are becoming better women. But my wife doubts it. Of course our village is particularly unfortunate, owing to that deplorable hotel. It has had such a bad influence. We had an extraordinary case before us on the Bench recently, connected with it.'

'That hotel did look too flash – it would attract the wrong crowd.'

'I've also had bother, bother, bother with the Rural District Council over the removal of tins, and another bother – a really maddening one – over a right of way through the church meadows. That almost made me lose my patience. And I really sometimes wonder whether I've been sensible in digging myself in in the country, and trying to make myself useful in local affairs. There is no gratitude. There is no warmth of welcome.'

'I quite believe it, Donaldson, and I know I'd never have a country place myself, even if the scenery is as pleasant as yours is, and even if I could afford it. I make do with a service flat in town, and I retain a small furnished cottage for my girls' holidays, and when they leave school I shall partly take them and partly send them abroad. I don't believe in undiluted England, nice as are sometimes the English. Shall we go up and have coffee?'

He ran up the staircase briskly, for he had found out what he wanted to know: Donaldson was feeling poor. He stuck him in a low leathern armchair, and had a look at him as he closed his eyes. That was it: he felt he couldn't afford his 'little place', and was running it down, so that no one should be surprised when he gave it up. Meanwhile, there was one point in the conversation it amused him to take up now that business was finished with: the reference to that 'extraordinary case' connected with the local hotel.

Donaldson opened his eyes when asked, and they had gone prawn-like. 'Oh, that was a case, it was a really really,' he said. 'I knew such things existed, of course, but I assumed in my innocence they were confined to Piccadilly. However, it has all been traced back to the hotel, the proprietress has had a thorough fright, and I don't think there will be any trouble in the future. Indecency between males.'

'Oh, good Lord!' said Sir Richard coolly. 'Black or white?'

'White, please, it's an awful nuisance, but I can't take black coffee now, although I greatly prefer it. You see, some of the hotel guests – there was a bar, and some of the villagers used to go in there after cricket because they thought it smarter than that charming old thatched pub by the church – you remember that old thatched pub. Villagers are terrific snobs, that's one of the disappointing discoveries one makes. The bar got a bad reputation of a certain type, especially at weekends, someone complained to the police, a watch was set, and the result was this quite extraordinary case… Really, really, I wouldn't have believed it. A little milk, please, Conway, if I may, just a little; I'm not allowed to take my coffee black.'

'So sorry. Have a liqueur.'

'No, no thanks, I'm not allowed that even, especially after lunch.'

'Come on, do – I will if you will. Waiter, can we have two double cognacs?'

'He hasn't heard you. Don't bother.'

Conway had not wanted the waiter to hear him, he had wanted an excuse to be out of the room and have a minute alone. He was suddenly worried in case that milkman had got into a scrape. He had scarcely thought about him since – he had a very full life, and it included an intrigue with a cultivated woman, which was gradually ripening – but nobody could have been more decent and honest, or more physically attractive in a particular way. It had been a charming little adventure, and a remarkably lively one. And their parting had been perfect. Wretched if the lad had come to grief! Enough to make one cry. He offered up a sort of prayer, ordered the cognacs, and rejoined Donaldson with his usual briskness. He put on the Renaissance armour that suited him so well, and 'How did the hotel case end?' he asked.

'We committed him for trial.'

'Oh! As bad as that?'

'Well, we thought so. Actually a gang of about half a dozen were involved, but we only caught one of them. His mother, if you please, is president of the Women's Institute, and hasn't had the decency to resign! I tell you, Conway, these people aren't the same flesh and blood as oneself. One pretends they are – but they aren't. And what with this disillusionment, and what with the right of way, I've a good mind to clear out next year, and leave the so-called country to stew in its own juice. It's utterly corrupt. This man made an awfully bad impression on the Bench and we didn't feel that six months, which is the maximum we were allowed to impose, was adequate to the offence. And it was all so revoltingly commercial – his only motive was money.'

Conway felt relieved; it couldn't be his own friend, for anyone less grasping...

'And another unpleasant feature – at least for me – is that he had the habit of taking his clients into my grounds.'

'How most vexatious for you!'

'It suited his convenience, and of what else should he think? I have a little wood – you didn't see it – which stretches up to the hotel, so he could easily bring people in. A path my wife was particularly fond of – a mass of bluebells in springtime – it was there they were caught. You may well imagine this has helped to put me off the place.'

'Who caught them?' he asked, holding his glass up to the light; their cognacs had arrived.

'Our local bobby. For we do possess that extraordinary rarity, a policeman who keeps his eyes open. He sometimes commits errors of judgement – he did on this occasion – but he's certainly observant, and as he was coming down one of the other paths, a public one, he saw a bright yellow shirt through the bracken – upsa! Take care!'

'Upsa!' were some drops of brandy, which Conway had spilt. Alas, alas, there could be no doubt about it. He felt deeply distressed, and rather guilty. The young man must have decided after their successful encounter to use the wood as a rendezvous. It was a cruel stupid world, and he was countenancing it more than he should. Wretched, wretched to think of that good-tempered, harmless chap being bruised and ruined... the whole thing so unnecessary – betrayed by the shirt he was so proud of... Conway was not often moved, but this time he felt much regret and compassion.

'Well, he recognised that shirt at once. He had particular reasons for keeping a watch on its wearer. And he got him, he got him. But he lost the other man. He didn't charge them straight away, as he ought to have done. I think he was genuinely startled and could scarcely believe his eyes. For one thing, it was so early in the morning – barely seven o'clock.'

'A strange hour!' said Conway, and put his glass down and folded his hands on his knee.

'He caught sight of them as they were getting up after committing the indecency, also he saw money pass, but instead of rushing in there and then he made an elaborate and totally unnecessary plan for interrupting the youth on the further side of my house, and of course he could have got him any time, any time. A stupid error of judgement. A great pity. He never arrested him until 7.45.'

'Was there then sufficient evidence for an arrest?'

'There was abundant evidence of a medical character, if you follow me – what a case, oh, what a case! – also there was the money on him, which clinched his guilt.'

'Mayn't the money have been in connection with his round?'

'No. It was a note, and he only had small change in connection with his round. We established that from his employer. But however did you guess he was on a round?'

'You told me,' said Conway, who never became flustered when he made a slip. 'You mentioned that he had a milk round and that the mother was connected with some local organisation which Mrs Donaldson takes an interest in.'

'Yes, yes, the Women's Institute. Well, having fixed all that up, our policeman then went on to the hotel, but it was far too late by that time, some of the guests were breakfasting, others had left, he couldn't go round cross-questioning everyone, and no one corresponded to the description of the person whom he saw being hauled up out of the fern.'

'What was the description?'

'An old man in pyjamas and a mackintosh – our Chairman was awfully anxious to get hold of him – oh, you remember our Chairman, Ernest Dray, you met him at my little place. He's determined to stamp this sort of thing out, once and for all. Hullo, it's past three, I must be getting back to my grindstone. Many thanks for lunch. I don't know why I've discoursed on this somewhat unsavoury topic. I'd have done better to consult you about the right of way.'

'You must another time. I did look up the subject once.'

'How about a spot of lunch with me this day week?' said Donaldson, remembering their business feud, and becoming uneasily jolly.

'This day week? Now can I? No, I can't. I've promised this day week to go and see my little girls. Not that they're little any longer. Time flies, doesn't it? We're none of us younger.'

'Sad but true,' said Donaldson, heaving himself out of the deep leather chair. Similar chairs, empty or filled with similar men, receded down the room, and far away a small fire smoked under a heavy mantelpiece. 'But aren't you going to drink your cognac? It's excellent cognac.'

'I suddenly took against it – I do indulge in caprices.' Getting up, he felt faint, the blood rushed to his head and he thought he was going to fall. 'Tell me,' he said, taking his enemy's arm and conducting him to the door, 'this old man in the mackintosh – how was it the fellow you caught never put you on his track?'

'He tried to.'

'Oh, did he?'

'Yes indeed, and he was all the more anxious to do so because we made it clear that he would be let off if he helped us to make the major arrest. But all he could say was what we knew already – that it was someone from the hotel.'

'Oh, he said that, did he? From the hotel.'

'Said it again and again. Scarcely said anything else, indeed almost went into a sort of fit. There he stood with his head thrown back and his eyes shut, barking at us. "Th'otel. Keep to th'otel. I tell you he come from th'otel." We advised him not to get so excited, whereupon he became insolent, which did him no good with Ernest Dray, as you may well imagine, and called the Bench a row of interfering bastards. He was instantly removed from the court and as he went he shouted back at us – you'll never credit this – that he and the old grandfather didn't mind it why should anyone else. We talked the case over carefully and came to the conclusion it must go to Assizes.'

'What was his name?'

'But we don't know, I tell you, we never caught him.'

'I mean the name of the one you did catch, the village boy.'

'Arthur Snatchfold.'

They had reached the top of the club staircase. Conway saw the reflection of his face once more in a mirror, and it was the face of an old man. He pushed Trevor Donaldson off abruptly, and went back to sit down by his liqueur glass. He was safe, safe, he could go forward with his career as planned. But waves of shame came over him. Oh for prayer! – but whom had he to pray to, and what about? He saw that little things can turn into great ones, and he did not want greatness. He was not up to it.

For a moment he considered giving himself up and standing his trial, however what possible good would that do? He would ruin himself and his daughters, he would delight his enemies, and he would not save his saviour. He recalled his clever man-oeuvres for a little fun, and the good-humoured response, the mischievous face, the obliging body. It had all seemed so trivial. Taking a notebook from his pocket, he wrote down the name of his lover, yes, his lover who was going to prison to save him, in order that he might not forget it. Arthur Snatchfold. He had only heard the name once, and he would never hear it again.

What Does It Matter?
A Morality

Before the civil war, Pottibakia was a normal member of the Comity of Nations. She erected tariff walls, broke treaties, persecuted minorities, obstructed at conferences unless she was convinced there was no danger of a satisfactory solution; then she strained every nerve in the cause of peace. She had an unknown warrior, a national salvo, commemorative postage-stamps, a characteristic peasantry, arterial roads; her emblem was a bee on a bonnet, her uniform plum-grey. In all this she was in line with her neighbours, and her capital city could easily be mistaken for Bucharest or Warsaw, and often was. Her president (for she was a republic) was Dr Bonifaz Schpiltz; Count Waghaghren (for she retained her aristocracy) being head of the police, and Mme Sonia Rodoconduco being Dr Schpiltz's mistress (for he was only human).

Could it be this liaison which heralded the amazing change – a change which has led to the complete isolation of a sovereign state? Presidents so often have mistresses, it is part of the constitution they have inherited from Paris, and Dr Schpiltz was an ideal president, with a long thin brown beard flecked with grey, and a small protuberant stomach. Mme Rodoconduco, as an actress and a bad one, also filled her part. She was extravagant, high-minded and hysterical, and kept Bopp (for thus all the ladies called him) on tenterhooks lest she did anything temperamental. She lived in a lovely villa on the shores of Lake Lago.

Now Count Waghaghren desired the President's downfall, and what the Count desired always came about, for he was powerful and unscrupulous. He desired it for certain reasons of *haute politique* which have been obscured by subsequent events – perhaps he was a royalist, perhaps a traitor or patriot, perhaps he was an emissary of that sinister worldwide Blue Elk organisation which is said to hold its sessions in the Azores. It is hopeless to inquire. Enough that he decided, as part of his scheme, to sow dissension between husband and wife. Mme Schpiltz's relatives were financiers, and a scandal was likely to start fluctuations on the exchange.

His plot was easily laid. He forged a letter from Mme Rodoconduco to Mme Schpiltz, inviting her to visit the lovely Villa Lago at a certain hour upon a certain day, he intercepted the reply of Mme Schpiltz accepting the invitation, and he arranged that the President and his mistress should be found in a compromising position at the moment of her call. All worked to perfection. The gendarme outside the villa omitted (under instructions) the national salvo when the President's wife drove up, the servants (bribed) conducted her as if by mistake to the Aphrodite bedroom, and there she found her husband in a pair of peach-blush pyjamas supported by Mme Rodoconduco in a lilac negligee.

Mme Rodoconduco went into hysterics, hoping they would gain her the upper hand. She shrieked and raved, while Count Waghaghren's microphone concealed under the lace pillows transmitted every tremor to his private cabinet. The President also played up. At first he pretended he was not there, then he rebuked his wife for interfering and his mistress for licentiousness, whereas he – he was a man, with a morality of his own. 'I am a man, ha ha!' and he tried folding his arms. Smack! He got one over the ear from Mme Rodoconduco for that. All was going perfectly except for the lack of cooperation on the part of Mme Schpiltz, who had started on entering the room and had said 'Bopp Bopp Bopp', but had then said no more. She watched the lovers without animosity and without amusement, occasionally showing concern when they struck one another but not caring to intervene. When there was a pause she said rather shyly, '*Madame – madame, j'ai faim,*'[1] and since the only reply was a stare she added, '*Vous m'avez invitée pour le goûter, n'est-ce-pas?*'[2]

'Certainly not, out of my house!' shrieked Mme Rodoconduco, but seeing a genuine look of disappointment on her visitor's face she said, 'Oh, very well, if you must eat you must.'

The servants now took Mme Schpiltz into another apartment, where *goûter* for two was already in evidence. She fell upon it, and Mme Rodoconduco followed her and sulkily did the honours. No allusion was made to the Aphrodite bedroom, the President had slipped away, and though the hostess was very nervous and therefore very rude she became easier in the presence of so much apathy, and they chatted on subjects of intellectual interest for quite a time.

The Count was unaccustomed to incidents without consequence and expected one lady or the other to come round to him in tears, or it might be the President himself asking him, as man to man, for advice in a little private difficulty. Then they would have fallen into his toils. But nothing happened. A few more officials and lackeys were in the know, but that was all. He must devise some other means of starting the ball rolling.

It may be remembered that there was a gendarme on duty that afternoon outside the Villa Lago. He, in the course of his usual dossier, reported that the President winked at him before driving away.

'Did you wink back?'

'Oh no, sir.'

The Count docked him a week's pay, and an order went out to all ranks that when the President of the Republic winked at them they were to wink back.

The order had no effect because it was based on a misconception. It is true that the President had winked as he drove away, but only because some dust blew in his eye. His thoughts were with the ladies at their *goûter*, not of gendarmes at all. Defeated by the subsequent steadiness of his gaze, Count Waghaghren reissued the order in a more drastic form: all ranks were to wink without waiting. This again had no effect. We do not see what we do not seek, and Dr Schpiltz, though a stickler for uniforms, was oblivious to all that passes inside them. It was his wife who enlightened him. 'Oh Bopp, how the poor policemen's eyes do twitch,' she remarked at a review. His attention once drawn, he observed that a twitch seemed to have become part of the national salvo. He did not like innovations about which he had not been consulted, and was about to issue a memorandum, when he noticed that the twitch was accompanied in some cases with a roguish smile. This put him on the right track. He had seen the same combination on the faces of little milliners and modistes of easy virtue, and he came to the only possible conclusion: the police were giving him the glad eye.

This called for a reprimand. But before drafting it he waited to make sure. There was no hurry – he could play cat and mouse if he liked, and he did get amusement at watching the forces of law and order playing futile tricks. He never winked back, oh no, he was always impassive and correct, besides, 'I am a man, aha, no danger in that quarter for *me*!' and he pulled at his thin brown beard. His drives through his capital city became more vivid, and he began to contrast the methods of superior and subordinate ranks. The way in which a peasant lad, fresh inside his uniform, would be half afraid to move his eyelid, and yet move it as if he could have moved much more, was indescribably droll. He became more and more entertained by his discovery, which not even his wife shared now, for she had a mind like a sieve and completely forgot the whole matter.

One day he happened to take a short constitutional in the Victory Park. This splendid park is a favourite resort of Pottibakians of all types, and it was his duty, as first citizen in the state, to walk there now and then. 'Look,' the people would say, 'there is the President walking round the bandstand! He is holding a newspaper in his hand, just as if he were you or me!

Marvellous!' But it was in a quieter part of the park that he suddenly encountered an incredibly good-looking mounted gendarme, and before he could stop himself had winked back. The man, who was very young, smiled charmingly, and pretended to have trouble with his horse. This led to a short conversation. There was not time for much, since the Bessarabian Minister was expected, but it included some presidential patting of the horse's neck, and a slight leaning forward on the part of its rider. 'Mirko, Your Excellency, Mirko Bolnovitch. Yes.' Which was all very well, but where? Not in the park, for God's sake, and he could not risk more tension with his wife. It is the pride of the Republic to house its president in prehistoric discomfort, and No. 100, Browning Street does not even possess a tradesman's entrance. The parlour is on the left of the door, the schoolroom on the right, and Mme Schpiltz or the young ladies see everyone who comes in. Not there, nor indeed anywhere. He withdrew hurriedly.

After his interview with the Bessarabian Minister he received a letter from Mme Rodoconduco. They had scarcely met since she boxed his ears, but it was tacitly understood that they were not to break. She wrote now on the deepest of black-edged paper, to make him part of the death of her brother, a realistic novelist to whom she was greatly attached. She must instantly repair to his estate, in case her nephews took a wrong view of the will. This, and the funeral, would detain her for at least a week, but as soon as she got back she much hoped to see her Bopp, and to apologise for her unfortunate warmth. On the whole not a bad letter. The woman wanted money – still, he had faced that long ago. She spoke of good taste and restraint – oh that she possessed them to the extent Mme Schpiltz did! – and she implied that though her mourning would be in good taste it could not be restrained. A *ménage à trois*: is it impossible when all three are rather exceptional? Finally she asked him a favour. All the servants at the

Villa Lago had been dismissed owing to their treachery, and she wanted someone to keep an eye on the new set in her absence. Would he be so very good as to pay a surprise visit one afternoon – Friday, say?

He replied pleasantly, condoled, enclosed a cheque, said he would look in at the villa next Friday at 3.00 on the pretext of having a bathe, hoped too for the possibilities of a *ménage à trois*. She replied to this from her family estate. His note had caught her just before starting, she said, she was deeply appreciative also for the enclosure, though the loss of a brother could never be repaired, and if only Mme Schpiltz could feel it possible to receive her some time... Then she spoke of the grief of the tenantry and the conduct of her nephews, correct hitherto, the arrangements in the little upland church, the hearse, the wreaths of Alpine flowers...

The Bessarabian affair still occupying him, he thought no more of Friday till his secretary reminded him. Then, punctually at 3.00, he drove up to the deserted villa. By chance his gendarme friend from the park was on guard. He had hardly given him a thought from that moment to this, but now it was as if he had been thinking of him all the time. He wanted to greet him, but it was impossible with the new major-domo bowing and inquiring whether he had done right in Madame la Baronne's absence to cover the sconces with brown holland. Turning away, he inspected the villa peevishly. He had never liked it less, and the Aphrodite bedroom was repellent. Was all this frou-frou and expense really necessary, as Sonia said it was, for love? She was always talking about love and sending in bills. He went out on to a balcony to get another glimpse of the mounted beauty, but the fellow looked in every direction but upwards, most exasperating, and the President dared not cough. Would Madame la Baronne desire the dining room suite re-upholstered in banana beige? Yes, if he knew her, she would. Then he said he must re-examine the hydrangeas in the porch. The gendarme kept absolutely still, a model of Pottibakian manhood, not winking now, all glorious in plum-grey. How grandly he sat his horse! Cheerful chatter, meant to embrace him, brought no smile to the strong lips. Alarmed by the fluting quality in his own voice, Dr Schpiltz withdrew, sharper set than ever. Now he would never know what happens when two men… and it might have been such a lesson with such a teacher… Well, well, he must just have his bathe and go, perhaps all's for the best.

Now the bathing room at the Villa Lago is a veritable triumph of Lido art. Divans and gymnastic apparatus mingle inseparably. It is accessible from the house and also on the lake side, where great sliding doors give access to marble steps leading down to Mme Rodoconduco's private beach. The view is beyond all description – poets have hymned it: rhododendrons, azaleas, bougainvillaeas, the blue waters of the lake, and on the farther side of it, just visible through the summer haze, the great rock of Praz, where the Pottibakians used to sacrifice their domestic animals before the introduction of Christianity. But the prospect gave the President no pleasure, not even when an aeroplane passed over it. Everything seemed worth just nothing at all. Holding up his swimming suit he prepared to step into it, when there was the sound of crunched pebbles, and the gendarme rode round the corner of the little bay, dismounted, strode clanging up the steps, took a gauntlet off, and shook hands.

The President frowned – often a sign of joy in the middle aged, and it was thus understood. 'Your Excellency – at your service. Now… My inspector has gone back to the city: he is a fool.' He pulled the sliding doors together and latched them. 'Excuse me…' He hung up his spiked helmet next to Mme Rodoconduco's hat. 'Excuse me again…' He unbuckled his holster. Sitting down on a settee, which was so soft that it made him laugh, he took his gaiters and boots off. 'Oh, I say, what a lovely room – better than the Victory Park.'

Dr Schpiltz could not speak. His mouth opened and shut like a bird's.

'Have you thought of me since?'

'Ye... yes.'

'I don't believe you. What is my name?'

The President could not remember.

'Mirko. Mirko Bolnovitch. Oh, I say!' He had noticed the parallel bars. 'That shall be my horse in here. Oh, I say!' He had seen the trapeze. Dr Schpiltz locked the door leading into the house. 'I'll do that, Your Excellency, don't you trouble.' And with a movement too rapid to follow he unlocked it. 'Now I'm in your power.'

'I think I'm in yours,' said the President, admiring him more boldly.

'I'm only eighteen. Shall we see?'

'You come from beyond Praz, don't you, Mirko?'

'Yes. How did you know? By my speech? Or by something else?' He continued to undress. The uniform lay neatly folded, official property. 'My singlet.' He drew it over his head. 'My shorts...'

'Well?'

'Well? Never content?' He stepped out of them smiling and sprang on to the trapeze. 'Do you like me up here?'

'You are much too far off!'

'Oh, but come up here, Your Excellency, join me!'

'No, thank you, Mirko, not at my age!'

'See, it's so easy, catch hold of whatever you like, only swinging.' The light filtered through high orange curtains on to loins and back. 'It is cooler with no clothes on,' he said. It did not seem to be. 'Now I have exercised all my muscles except...' He was sitting astride the parallel bars.

The President of the Republic approached his doom. Deftly, as he did so, was his pince-nez twitched off his nose. 'Now you can't see how ugly I am.'

'Mirko, you ugly...' He tottered into the trap and it closed on him.

'Aie, you're in too much of a hurry,' laughed the young man. 'Come up and do exercises with me first. Business before pleasure.'

'I'd rather not, I shall fall, my dear boy.'

'Oh no you won't, dearest boyest.'

Contrary to his better judgement, Dr Schpiltz now ascended the parallel bars. He became more and more involved. Heaven knew what he had to pass through, how he was twisted about and pinched. He felt like a baby monkey scratched and mismanaged on the top of a lofty tree. The science of the barrack-room, the passions of the stables, the primitive instincts of the peasantry, the accident of the parallel bars and Dr Schpiltz's quaint physique – all combined into something quite out of the way, and as it did so the door opened and Mme Rodoconduco came into the room, followed by the Bessarabian Minister.

'We have here...' she was saying.

Neither of them heard her.

'We have here... we have...'

The Bessarabian Minister withdrew. Mirko, alerted, relaxed a grip and they fell off the bars on to a mattress. Mme Rodoconduco was so thunderstruck that she could not even scream. She remained in a sort of frenzied equilibrium, and when she did speak it was in ordinary tones. She said, 'Bopp, oh Bopp, Bopp!'

He heard that, and raised a lamentable goatee. 'You Jezebel! Why aren't you at the funeral?' he hissed.

'Whose funeral?' cried she in flame-coloured taffeta, Titian-cut.

'Your brother's.'

'Alekko's? He's alive.'

'How dare you contradict me? He's dead. Oh, oh… You've written to me about his funeral twice.'

'I never did, Bopp, never.' Distracted, she picked up a bath towel and threw it over the pair. They looked better as a heap.

'Disgraceful! Incredible! And I wrote back and sent you a cheque for the mourning.'

'I have received no cheque,' she cried. 'Here's something gravely amiss.'

'Yes, all you think of is cheques! What are you here for now?'

'Why, your telephone call,' she replied with tears in her eyes. 'You rang me up this morning to be here at 3.30 in case the Bessarabian Minister called.'

'I never rang you up. More lies.'

'You did, dear, you did really, I answered the call myself and the Minister said you had rung him up also.'

'The Minister? Good God! When is he coming?'

'He has come and has gone.'

'Not – oh Sonia, not – '

'Yes, and his wife was with him, to see the view, and this is the view they saw. My villa. My Villa Lago. Well, this is the end of my career, such as it is. I can never go back to the stage.'

'I am likely never to leave it,' said Dr Schpiltz slowly. 'I shall go down to history as the president who – oh, what can even the historians say? I shall resign tomorrow, but that will be the beginning, not the end. Could I get over the frontier? Would an aeroplane? However did you open the door?'

'It was unlocked.'

'Unlocked? I locked it myself.'

'I think we must both be bewitched,' she said, shading her eyes. She was behaving wonderfully well, she was one of those women who behave alternately well and badly. The President began to be convinced of her sincerity and to feel ashamed.

'I know that *I* have been. Whatever has possessed me? When I look round' – and he thrust his head out of the towel – 'when I think what I was an hour ago, I begin to wonder, Sonia, whether those old fairy tales you used to recite may not be true, whether men cannot be changed into beasts…'

'Ah,' she interrupted, catching sight of the spiked helmet hanging beside her hat, 'I've seen the whole thing! We've got Waghaghren here.'

'Well, hardly,' he demurred.

'It's one of his traps.'

'Trap? But how should he set one?'

'Who knows how or why the Count does things? We only know he does them. Now are you absolutely sure you locked the door into the villa?'

'Absolutely, because this lad – because he – ' He broke off and cried, 'Mirko! You're not here under orders, are you?'

Mirko lay on the mattress half a-dreaming, drowsy with delight. He had carried out the instructions of his superior officer, gratified a nice old gentleman and had a lovely time himself. He could not understand why, when the President's question was repeated, he should get a kick. He laughed and made the reply on which the whole history of Pottibakia turns. If he had said 'Yes, I am here under orders,' or if, acting under orders, he had said 'No,' his country would still be part of the Comity of Nations. But he made the reply which is now engraved on his statue. He said, 'What does it matter?'

'You will soon learn whether it matters,' said the President. 'Sonia, please ring the bell.' Mme Rodoconduco stopped him, 'No, do not ring. We suffer too much from distant communications. I must question him myself, I see.' She raised her eyes to the trapeze. 'You! You down on the floor, you have admitted to His Excellency that you are an *agent provocateur*?'

Propping his chin on his fists, Mirko answered, 'Gracious lady, I am. But His Excellency acts provokingly too. When I netted him in the park I thought to myself, "This will be fun." And I am a peasant, and we peasants never think a little fun matters. You and His Excellency and the head of the police know better, but we peasants have a proverb: "Poking doesn't count".'

'And pray what does that mean?'

'Oh, never mind, Sonia, don't question him. You belong to such different worlds.'

'You should know what poking means, lady, if half the tales about you are true. Anyhow, it is a religious story about the Last Judgement.'

'We are freethinkers, religion means nothing to us,' said the President, but Mirko continued,

'At the Last Judgement the Pottibakians were in a terrible fright, because they had all done something which all three of us have done and hope to do again. There they were going up in a long line, the nobility like you going first, the people of my sort waiting far behind. We waited and waited and presently heard a loud cheering up at the Gate. So we sent a messenger to find out what had happened, and he came back shouting all down the line, "Hooray! Hooray! Poking doesn't count." And why should it? Do you understand now?'

'I understand that you are the lowest of the low, or the Count would not employ you,' said she. 'Will you be so good as to insert that remark of mine into your report?'

'No need, gracious lady, a microphone is already installed.'

'Where?' gasped the President.

'These new servants would know. That major-domo is a government electrician.'

'Then has all I said been heard?'

'Yes, and all the strange noises you made. Still, what does it matter? It was fun. Oh, some things matter, of course, the crops, and the vintage matters very much, and our glorious Army, Navy and Air Force, and fighting for our friends, and baiting the Jews, but isn't that all? Why, in my village where everyone knows one another and the priest is worst... Why, when my uncle needed a goat...'

But here the door opened again and Mme Schpiltz entered the room. Dressed in alpaca and a home-made toque, she presented an equal contrast to her husband's bath towel, to Mme Rodoconduco's Venetian splendours, and to the naked gendarme. As on her previous visit, she was greeted with torrents of talk and knew not how to reply. 'Madame, madame,' wailed her hostess, 'we are ruined,' and beneath her full-bosomed lamentations could be heard the President's plaintive pipe: 'Oh Charlotte, I have been fatally indiscreet. Why did you come?'

'Because you telephoned to me.'

'I telephoned to you? Never!'

'But what has happened? You have only been bathing.'

'Madame, madame, do not ask him further, it is something too awful, something he could never explain, something which even I... and which you with your fine old-world outlook, your nobility, your strictness of standard... Oh madame... and in my villa too, after all your previous goodness to me... my Villa Lago... But you have influence in high financial circles, use it at once before it is too late, let us fly to a cottage *à trois* before the Count – what am I saying? The Count not only heard but he hears! Count Waghaghren!' She whirled her arms in every direction. 'Somewhere, a microphone!'

'But I like the wireless so much as long as I have something to do at the same time,' said Mme Schpiltz.

'Charlotte! We have reason to believe that a microphone has been secretly installed here, and that the Count can hear everything in his private cabinet.'

'But why shouldn't he hear everything? I think that's such a nice idea. He is such a clever man, I knew his poor grandmother well. I remember him saying when he was quite a tiny tot, "Me want to hear evvyfing", and we saying "No, baby dear, baby can't ever do that", but he knew and we didn't, for thanks to this wonderful invention he can. How like him!'

'He has probably installed television too.'

'How like him again! He always used to say, "Me peepy-weep", and now he can. Really I do think science… But can no one tell me what has happened?'

'I could,' said Mirko.

'Charlotte, don't speak to that man! I forbid it!'

'Excuse me, Bopp, I shall speak to him; besides, judging by those clothes over on the divan, he seems to be a policeman, and so the proper person. Well, my man?'

'Lady, do you in God's name know what poking is?'

'But of course. There would be no babies without it. But naturally.'

'Thank heaven for that! Well, His Excellency wanted to poke me but did not know how, so I showed him.'

'And is that the whole story?'

'Yes.'

'Young man, you didn't hurt my husband with rough jokes, I hope?'

'Only in ways he enjoyed.'

'And are you yourself satisfied?'

'Not yet. I want to show him again.'

'For that you will have to wait. Thank you.' She dismissed him and turned to the others. 'Well, there we are at last. I thought that someone had been hurt, and it's simply that two people – yes, one doesn't talk about these things of course, but really – what do they matter?'

'Ah!' cried Mirko, 'here is someone at last who says what I do. What does it matter?' And he shouted out the cry which was soon to rend the nation asunder, shouted it with such force and, as it happened, so close to the microphone that Count Waghaghren fell senseless.

'What does it matter? Well, that's one way of looking at it, I suppose,' said Mme Rodoconduco, examining her fingernails.

'It's the only way,' pronounced the President. 'It's essential to a stable society. But no government has ever thought of it, and we've learned it too late.'

They were not too late, because the Count remained unconscious for the rest of the day. A master plotter, he left no one to carry on his plans, and by the time he came to himself the famous Manifesto had been drafted and affixed to the principal public buildings in the capital. Its wording was as follows,

> Fellow Citizens! Since all of you are interested in the private lives of the great, we desire to inform you that we have all three of us had carnal intercourse with the President of the Republic, and are hoping to repeat it.
>
> > Charlotte Schpiltz (housewife)
> > Sonia Rodoconduco (artiste)
> > Mirko Bolnovitch (gendarme)

There was some discussion as to the wording of the Manifesto. Mme Rodoconduco wanted some reference to the overmastering and ennobling power of love, Mirko something more popular. Both were overruled. The Manifesto appeared in the evening papers, and led to questions both in the Senate and the Chamber of Deputies. The Ministry could not answer the questions and resigned. The President then drove down in state and addressed both houses. He began by paying a glowing tribute to Count Waghaghren, whose organisation had now reached such a pitch that not only the private actions of each citizen but even his or her thoughts would soon be recorded automatically. 'I intend therefore,' he went on, 'to form a Ministry of all the Morals, which can alone survive such scrutiny, and as soon as it is in office its first duty will be to depose me. Once deposed, I shall be liable to arrest and to prosecution under our Criminal Code, the most admirable, as we often agreed, in Eastern Europe. Or it may be that I shall not be prosecuted at all, but dealt with summarily, like one of the signatories to the Manifesto, who has been sent for six years to the mines, on the charge of deserting his horse. The other two signatories are at large for the moment, but should not long remain so.'

The scenes at the conclusion of his speech were indescribable, particularly in the Senate, where old men got up and poured out their confessions for hours, and could not be stopped. The Chamber of Deputies kept a stiffer upper lip, and there were cries of 'Flogging's too good!' and fain counter-cries of 'Flog me!' No one dared to take office, owing to the President's un-measured eulogy of the police, and he continued to govern as dictator until the outbreak of the civil war.

He is now dictator again, but since all the states, led by Bessarabia, have broken off diplomatic relations it is extremely difficult to get Pottibakian news. Visas are refused, and the inter-national express traverses the territory behind frosted glass. Now and then a postcard of the Bolnovitch Monument falls out of an aeroplane, but unlike most patriotic people the Pottibakians appear to be self-contained. They till the earth and have become artistic, and are said to have developed a fine literature which deals very little with sex. This is puzzling, as is the indissolubility of marriage – a measure for which the Church has vainly striven elsewhere. Gratified by her triumph, she is now heart and soul with the nation, and the Archimandrite of Praz has reinterpreted certain passages of scripture, or has pronounced them corrupt. Much here is obscure, links in the argument have been denied to us, nor, since we cannot have access to the novels of Alekko, can we trace the steps by which natural impulses were converted into national assets. There seem, however, to have been three stages: first the Pottibakians were ashamed of doing what they liked, then they were aggressive over it, and now they do as they like. There I must leave them. We shall hear little of them in the future, for the surrounding powers dare not make war. They hold – and perhaps rightly – that the country has become so infectious that if it were annexed it would merely get larger.

And what of the Count? Some rumours have come through. He fought in the civil war, was taken prisoner, and his punishment had to be decided. Mirko wanted him sent to the mines, Sonia flogged, the President banished, but Mme Schpiltz was the cruellest of all. 'Poor man, I can't see what he has done,' she said. 'Do let him keep on doing it.' Her advice was taken, and the Count was reinstated in his former office, which has been renamed the Lunatic Asylum, and of which he is the sole inmate. Here he sits all alone amid the latest apparatus, hearing, seeing, tasting and smelling through his fellow citizens, and indexing the results. On public holidays his private cabinet (now his cell) is thrown open, and is visited by an endless queue of smiling Pottibakians, who try to imagine the old days when that sort of thing mattered, and emerge laughing.

The Classical Annex

The Municipal Museum at Bigglesmouth was badly off for Greek and Roman stuff, and the Curator rather neglected what was known as the Classical Annex. So imagine his guilty conscience when one dark afternoon, just as the museum was closing, the custodian came to his office with news of a breakage there. It was like hearing of the death of a worthy but tedious relative. 'Not the Early Christian sarcophagus?' he inquired, secretly hoping that it might be.

No, not the sarcophagus nor the nude neither, no, only minor objects.

'Objects? What? More than one breakage?'

'Well, sir, to be quite frank it's a couple of terracotta items in Wall Case A.'

'Not the Tanagra statuette?' he cried with increasing emotion.

The custodian hastened to assure him that one of the items was not the Tanagra – everyone knew how valuable she was. The other, on the other hand, was.

'The best thing in the room – the only good thing in it. How on earth did it happen? Were you leaning on the case? Were you pointing her out to the public?'

The custodian waxed indignant. Most certainly he had not been pointing her out to the public. There never was any public in the Classical Annex.

'When did the accident happen?'

'I couldn't say, sir.'

'Oh, couldn't you? That means you haven't been going your rounds properly.'

Having silenced all criticism, except what came from his own conscience, the Curator snatched up his keys and went to inspect. Crossing the entrance hall of the museum, with frieze entitled Motherly Love, he passed the unique series of wooden churns discovered in the bed of the Biggle, and the reconstruction of the Town Pump. Modern Art opened behind that. Beyond Modern

Art was the Classical Annex. It was by far the least attractive room in the museum – stuffy, badly lit, and not too clean. He unlocked Wall Case A. Alas and alas! The Tanagra, a charming little girl, had fallen, pedestal and all, and chipped her pretty hat. The other statuette – a bearded Etruscan thing – had suffered even more, but this did not signify, as the City Council had been told that he was bad.

'You can go now, I will let myself out,' he told the custodian, 'and you had better think over what you propose to say to the Committee on Thursday. See! There is dust on the arm of the male statuette. He must have been broken for days.'

Alone in the museum, he examined the wall case carefully, and discovered several further breakages. A small plaque representing a nymph had cracked, and an Apis bull had slid towards it, toppling on to its nose. Misfortunes tended to come in pairs – and as for the two terracottas it was almost as if they had picked their way to their common doom. With delicate fingers he tidied up the shelves, and was about to take the damaged objects to his office, and consider how best they might be repaired, when there was a tinkle behind him. The fig leaf attached to the nude in the centre of the room had fallen on to the floor.

'Really, the things might be alive,' he grumbled, picking it up. It was a veritable giant among fig leaves, the work of a local ironmonger. He did not like to leave it for the charwoman to find it in the morning – employees at Bigglesmouth were easily upset. Owing to its weight, it had chafed through the suspending circlet of string. The nude, now wholly so for the first time, was a worthless late Roman work, and represented an athlete or gladiator of the non-intellectual type. He had never liked it, and had reported strongly against purchasing it, and he liked it less than ever in the twilight that began to invade the dingy museum. The City Fathers had wanted something life-sized and cheap, 'and they've got 'em both, by gad' he murmured, climbing fastidiously upon a chair, with the fig leaf swinging from a new piece of string, and thinking how much more personable was his own son Denis than this classical lout.

'Scrap heap's the place for you,' he said, as he embraced the stone buttocks and fastened the string above them. 'Broken up for road metal – that's all you're worth.' Stepping down, he gazed at his handiwork. The fig leaf didn't hang right – tilted out unsuitably. He quite lost his temper. Why should his time be wasted over all this rubbish? And clenching his fist he hit it hard. It fell into position with a ping. Dusting his hands against one another, he went back to the two statuettes.

He had put them for safety on the plush couch, at least a foot apart. Now they lay together, and, queerer still, appeared to have stuck. He had never known terracottas stick before – probably the result of the damp Bigglesmouth climate – and he felt quite despairful – everything he turned his back on seemed to go wrong. Would he never get home to his tea? As he bent down to separate them, he heard a string snap, and the fig leaf whizzed across the room. It might have killed him. 'Damn and blast you, that's too much,' he cried, then shrieked, and leapt into the Early Christian sarcophagus. He was not an instant too soon. The nude had cracked off its pedestal and was swaying to fall on him.

With rare presence of mind, the Curator made the sign of the Cross, and the Classical Annex and all its contents became instantly still. It might have been a dream but for an obscene change in the statue's physique. He gazed from his asylum in horror. He glanced at the fig leaf, now all too small. He backed away from it, crossing himself constantly, he could still see it from Modern Art, it was even prominent from among the oaken churns, he did not lose sight of it until he sidled under Motherly Love. Then he ran – yes, he did run. He let himself out of the museum, not forgetting to lock it carefully behind him as you may well imagine, then he rushed over Coronation Square and down Bonfire Street, where he boarded a municipal tram.

The Curator was no materialist, like too many savants of the nineteenth century. Oxford had taught him to admit the supernatural willingly, and he wasted no time in indignation or brooding. As soon as his natural terror subsided and one particular apparition ceased to threaten him, he began to think what should be done. Clearly something was loose in the Classical Annex, some obscene breath from the past, and it might not be impossible to convince the City Fathers of this, for they were God-fearing men. They did not really care for Greek and Roman stuff, and had only been tempted to the nude by its cheapness. 'You never know where young people may not pick up dirty thoughts,' Councillor Bodkin had said, when they sent the order to the ironmonger. Once get them impressed and all would be easy. His best plan, he decided, would be to close the museum on his own authority, and wire for one or two friends of his, eminent experts, whose names would intimidate the Mayor. Sir Newton Surtees the great speleologist, Canon Bootle Anderson who exposed the behaviourists, Dame Lucy Ironside, president of the Self-Health Association and organiser of the World Retention Movement – these were not inconsiderable figures, and their outlook was his own. In their presence the museum should be unsealed. If nothing was found – and he was well aware how impish the powers of darkness can be – he would resign his post and they would find him a new one. If anything was found, steps should be taken to exorcise the town and to dispose of the nude as a Priapus to some connoisseur.

It was night when he left the tram, but the walk down Michaelmas Avenue held no terrors for him. He had thought the thing out, with a mind both powerful and modern, and wiping his spectacles he looked calmly into the lighted doorway of his residence, and into the pale blue eyes of his wife.

'Hullo, dear, where's Denis?' she said.

'Denis? I don't know.'

'He went to meet you.'

'Did he? I must have passed him in the tram.'

'You don't usually take the tram. What a nuisance, now he will probably rush all the way down, foolish boy, and he's practically nothing on but his football shorts. They've won that match and he wanted to tell you.'

'Well, when he's rushed down he'll rush back.'

'Unless he looks for you in the museum.'

'He can scarcely do that,' said the Curator quietly. 'The museum is locked up.'

'Oh yes he can, dear. He snatched up your duplicate keys. I couldn't stop him. He's getting awfully headstrong and excitable – dear, whatever's the matter?'

'Nothing.' He rang the museum up and got Number Unobtainable. While his wife was preparing tea, he slipped out of the house. He reminded himself that it was only a statue, and a debased one right away in the Classical Annex, where Denis was unlikely to go. He compelled himself to keep calm, while running at full speed up Michaelmas Avenue and down Bonfire Street, until he was again in Coronation Square.

The museum squatted on the margin like a toad. He inserted a key into its skin, oilily, and it received him. None of the lights were on, which gave him hope. Then far away he heard a familiar, an adorable sound: a giggle. Denis was laughing at something. He dared not call out or give any sign, and crept forward cautiously, guiding himself by well-known objects, like the oaken churns, until he heard his son say, 'Aren't you awful?' and there was the sound of a kiss. Gladiatorial feints, post-classical suctions, a brute planning its revenge. There was not a moment to lose, and as the giggling started again and soared up into hysterics against a ground-bass of grunts the

Curator stepped into the Christian sarcophagus and made the sign of the Cross. Again it worked. Once more the Classical Annex and all its contents became still.

Then he switched on the light.

And in after-years a Hellenistic group called The Wrestling Lesson became quite a feature at Bigglesmouth, though it was not exhibited until the Curator and the circumstances of his retirement were forgotten. 'Very nice piece, very decent' was Councillor Bodkin's opinion. 'Look 'ow the elder brother's got the little chappie down. Look 'ow well the little chappie's taking it.'

The Torque

The little basilica was crammed. Perpetua sat to the left of the altar, robed in white. Through a thin veil her commanding nose and fastidious mouth could be clearly seen. She never moved, her eyes fixed ecstatically upon the god-head. Below her, on plainer chairs, sat her father and mother, Justus and Lucilla, landowners of substance, her young brother Marcian, and her little sisters, Galla and Justa. To the right of the altar, overbalancing the domestic group, towered the ecclesiastics: the Bishop of the district, the lesser clergy, the father confessors, and several solitaries who had been attracted by the strangeness and special sanctity of the event. The body of the church was filled with neighbours, the faithful and the curious. It was richly decorated in a rustic fashion, and above the altar, like a trophy, hung a barbaric torque of gold. Through the open western door Justus's farmyard could be seen. It too was full of people – slaves, husbandmen, soldiers. These last were all baptised Christians and particularly devout. They had been drafted in to protect the sacred ceremony from interference. The district was not as settled as it had been. Deceitfully now did it sleep in the autumn sunlight – the vineyards, the cornlands, the olive yards, the low ridges of the hills. The soldiers glanced occasionally at the hills.

Mass had been said. Lucilla, a little drowsy, awoke with a start. The great ceremony of her daughter's dedication was to begin. Perpetua Virgo, perpetual virginity. She nudged her husband and he awoke frowning. For he had promised the Bishop to build a bigger, better basilica as a thank-offering, also Perpetua's dowry had to be surrendered to the Heavenly Bridegroom, and Marcian's heritage impaired, and the little girls go almost unportioned. He had not expected this. He had hoped to marry his eldest daughter to some substantial farmer. There had been little talk of dedicated virgins when he was young, and he had never expected to rear one in the family. The animals mated – he could hear them at it when the chanting ceased – and are we not like them in that? Still frowning, he took his wife's hand ritually, then dropped it, for the Bishop had begun his address.

Standing beside the altar, the Bishop reminded his congregation that this dedication would in any case have taken place and been blessed, but it was now signalised by a miracle which would live in the annals of the Church for ever. Five days ago, as they all knew, the virgin Perpetua had set forth on a journey, not from idleness, not from wantonness, not from a desire to see the world (which she already too well knew), but to confer with a holy matron of her acquaintance upon religious matters. She travelled in all seemliness, with her brother as escort and a suitable retinue of slaves. Edifying was the meeting between the two devout females, long did they converse, many were the pious propositions they exchanged. Presently came the hour for her return to her parents' abode. She mounted her mule, her brother rode somewhat behind as was suitable, her retinue followed on foot. The evening was calm, the air balmy, no danger seemed to menace. But these are the moments when the Adversary is most active. She turns a corner of the road and –

'Oh my brethren oh my sisters, what did our virgin then see? Horsemen. What horsemen? Goths. She shrieks, she trembles, they bear down on her, Goths, Goths, hideous of form and of face, they are here. They lay hold of Perpetua and hale her off her mule, they clasp her, my brethren my sisters, she is lost. Is she not lost? It seems so. Her brother is overpowered, for he is but a stripling, her retinue scattered. With their booty the Goths, yes the Goths I again say, ride onward into the hills. They have captured that which is more precious than gold or jewels, namely a virgin, Perpetua the virgin whom the whole world could not ransom.

'What are they going to do to her, oh my brethren oh my sisters, what?

'Night falls, they come to a miserable hut. Wine is offered to Perpetua which she spurns and they drink and there is an orgy. She is thrown to the ground. And one of them – he who once wore this golden circlet above our altar and now wears it no longer – nay nay I cannot continue – '

He paused, and there was silence in the basilica except for sore swallowings in throats. Using the frank language of his age, the language of St Augustine and St Jerome, he continued as follows,

' – and loosens his own. To lose her virginity to the husband for whom she was once destined would be for Perpetua defilement enough, but this! The ravisher covers her, his hot breath beats back her prayers, and his member – and they are membered like horses…'

He paused again and somebody laughed. He started with anger and amazement, and the congregation trembled. Who had laughed? They looked right and left, and lo! the face of Marcian the virgin's young brother was crimson.

For a few moments the service of dedication stopped. Marcian gulped and gasped, and his features returned towards their former colour. His parents bent over him, his mother asked him whether he was ill. He shook his head. He was a modest boy, in awe of his sister as they all were, and his conduct was inexplicable. He now sat with his head bowed and his thick lips closed – there was a strain of African blood in the family and it had come out in Marcian.

The Bishop looked at him and hesitated. He suspected diabolical possession, and the lower clergy were crossing themselves right and left. Perpetua alone was undisturbed. Her eyes remained fixed on the altar ecstatically. She was far away from such trifles. And taking his cue from her he decided to resume his homily as if nothing had happened.

Let them note (he said) that at that supreme moment when all seemed lost the virgin's prayer was heard. There was a lightning flash, the Goth staggered back and fell as though struck to the ground. Nay more, he was visited with repentance and followed her humbly when she departed, and offered her as atonement that great golden torque that lay against the altar now. She returned home unscathed and triumphant, *virgo victrix*.[3] She had done what the might of men cannot. And in due time, he doubted not, she would subdue all around her to her holy purpose, and the foul engendering which is Adam's curse would cease.

He looked at Justus and Lucilla as he spoke these last words, and they looked away. It was in sin that they had engendered Perpetua, and in sin – greater sin – Marcian. Much pleasure had gone to the making of Marcian. This, they now learned, is wrong. All fruitfulness and warmth are wrong. They tried to understand this and looked humbly at their formidable daughter, who alone could save them from eternal punishment. When the dedication was over they asked Marcian what had made him laugh. 'I do not know, something I was not thinking of made me laugh,' was his reply.

'It may harm us, that laugh of yours.'

'I am sorry, dear father, I will try to laugh no more. But the cattle need driving in. The country is unsafe with Goths about. May I now go and help the herdsmen?'

'No, for there now has to be Holy Converse in the barn,' said Lucilla with a sigh. 'All must repair there.'

They did so. The barn resembled the basilica, except that Perpetua now spoke. She exhorted all present to follow her example, the females particularly, and fixed her beady eyes upon her sisters, Galla and Justa, merry little maidens. Males, she explained, were of coarser clay, hewers of wood and drawers of water, and could achieve less. The Bishop took her up a little here. Males, he asserted, could also achieve virginity and must be encouraged to do so. The involuntary pollutions which sometimes overcame them were from the Devil certainly, but not fatal. He appealed – and here his eye fixed Marcian – to men and particularly to youths in the first tumult of their ripeness.

'He is a good boy,' said his father.

'He is the comfort of our old age,' said his mother. And little Galla and Justa piped up, 'We like Marcian. Oh, we like Marcian much better than Perpetua. He makes us toys.'

The Bishop threw up his hands in annoyance. 'Toys? Toys? O generation of vipers, who will save you from the wrath to come? It is she, she alone, that virgin who consents to sojourn amongst you, she alone averts the merited thunderbolt.' These were strong words, but he had been disturbed by the unseemly interruption in the basilica and was half-minded to pronounce an exorcism now. But there seemed insufficient evidence, so he terminated the Converse and proceeded to his bullock-cart. All accompanied him with the exception of Marcian, who exploded once more into laughter. For he, and he alone, knew how Perpetua's virginity had been preserved.

It had been preserved as follows.

That day, five days ago, when they met the Goths, he had set forth without forebodings. Attendance on Perpetua was part of his duty, he was humble and loyal and ready to die for her if necessary. She spoke little to him on the journey out, if she did so he rode forward to receive her orders and fell back to transmit them to the slaves. He did not ask himself whether he liked her – it would have been an unseemly question – but he knew that he lay under her continuous and permanent displeasure. For some years ago he had been guilty of impurity. One of his mother's house-girls had given him a thrill which he still remembered. His mother had beaten the girl, his father had laughed, all was passing off normally when Perpetua had a sort of fit. She called them all to her couch, and made him promise he would never be unchaste again. It was easy to promise, for he was thoroughly frightened, and being only thirteen assumed that his carnal impulses would weaken. She knew better. She had been waiting for such an opportunity as this, and she began to organise a holy spy-system with the help of the monks who began to haunt the farm. All was done in the name of his parents, and they were watched too, and gradually the ease went out of life. It was the price they paid for rearing a saint.

Brother and sister made a striking pair as they rode into the entangling hills – she severe, ascetic, veiled, he open to all the winds and suns of heaven, his knees and neck bare until she reminded him to cover them. Once he started a countrified song which the retinue took up, but she stopped that and substituted a psalm. When they reached their destination he had to remain outside it, for so holy was the matron that no male creature was suffered to enter her abode. Even male mosquitoes were prohibited, the slaves said. They became ribald on the subject, and he had to check them while not wanting to do so. 'Tell your mistress that it is time we left, for the sun falls towards the hills,' he told them presently. A slave passed the message through a grille to an aged woman, and after further delay Perpetua appeared.

She was even graver than before, but more disposed to talk. When they had started for home she summoned him and told him that she was now decided on perpetual virginity.

'It is God's will, sister.'

'I shall not retire to the desert. The matron has counselled me otherwise. I shall make my abode amongst you.'

'It is evidently God's will – sister, look at that hawk.'

'What of it?'

'Someone has disturbed him.'

'Marcian, when will you learn seemliness?'

'Have I not? I do try.'

'I was about to speak to your edification, but you are diverted by the passing flight of a bird.'

At this moment the Goths appeared. There were only three of them, and had Perpetua kept quiet the two parties might have ridden past each other with friendly salutation. But she lifted up her voice and prayed. 'O Lord God of Hosts O God of Abraham Isaac and Jacob deliver us out of the hands of our enemies,' she cried. Her prayer was heard by the slaves and they started to run away. The Goths chased the slaves. One of them, pressing by Marcian, nicked his horse on the rump with a knife. The horse reared and he fell off. Seeing him tumble, another Goth haled Perpetua off her mule. The disaster was immediate and complete. Brother and sister bit the dust while the squeals of their retinue grew fainter and the sun dropped towards the hills with a jerk.

Further indignities followed. His ankles were bound, he was made to hop so that he fell down again amidst loud laughter, a barbarian spat in his face, another threw an overripe fig, he was flung crossways on his mount, Perpetua replaced on hers, getting pinched in the process, and then they all rode deeper into the hills. They came to a hut, a sort of storehouse, for plunder lay about, including a barrel of wine. The captives were dismounted and Marcian's ankles freed. He began to look around him. One of them appeared to the leader, for he gave orders and wore a magnificent torque of gold. Perpetua was engaged in prayer. He tried to comfort her, but could not gain her attention.

'Sister, I do not think we are in great danger. They seem to mean us no harm, though I cannot follow their speech. They want our mounts perhaps, not ourselves. I do not think they want us at all. They are only wild boys who do not know their own wishes or what is in their hearts.'

'O God of Abraham Isaac and Jacob deliver us.'

'Amen and I am sure he will. They are forgetting us, and soon we shall be able to walk away. I may even untether your mule so that you can escape in comfort.'

'O God…'

'And look, they are preparing food.'

'Food, brother?' The suggestion outraged her. 'Unholy food.'

'It has been stolen from holy people by the look of it.'

'It is the fouler for that.'

'Sister, I must confess I am hungry.' For an animal had broken loose inside him. 'You had delicate refreshment at the matron's, I was offered nothing. With respect I must eat.' And walking boldly to the trestle where the Goths were at work he pointed to himself and said 'Marcian', and pointed to the man with the torque, who said 'Euric', and everyone laughed. The faces of the barbarians were frank, childish and powerful. Emotions passed over them like clouds. No one, not even themselves, knew what they would do next. Having given him their best, they drank to him and to each other and to the Majesty of Rome. And they drank to Perpetua and explored her contours with bold blue eyes. She fell on her knees, not the safest of positions. One of them licked his lips, another fingered his breeks, and suddenly all five were struggling on the floor. All five, for Marcian had intervened to save her. The confusion was terrible. Ten arms, five heads and ten legs got mixed into a revolving ball whence the shrieks of the virgin and the howls of her ravishers floated out into the night. 'Sister, escape,' Marcian repeated. 'I will hold them off from you. Escape.' She escaped and he got raped.

The surprise exceeded the pain. 'Not me, this can't be for me' was his thought as the notorious Gothic embrace penetrated. Women died from it, the story went. That seed was said to breed devils. 'Well, scarcely in my case.' The idea made him laugh, and he heard Euric laugh. For it had been Euric.

So like these Goths! Food and drink, lechery, sleep, fighting, food, mirth, drink, boy, girl, no difference. Euric rolled off him when satisfied and could easily have been killed. But one does not kill beasts or babies. And the other two were no longer dangerous. The force of example had proved too strong for them. Call themselves devils, did they? He knew better. What had happened was not serious. The discomfort was already passing off and no one need know.

He hurried after his sister, found her at prayer, set her on her mule and tried to bestride his horse. A warning twinge deterred him, so he walked instead and led his precious charge down the mountain. The moon had risen and revealed landmarks he recognised. For a time she was well content and sang psalms of deliverance, but when her heart was emptied she addressed him with asperity and chid him for his ill-handling of the expedition. He did not defend himself – he had scarcely reached the age of defence – and certainly he ought not to have fallen off his horse when Goths arrived. Still, he felt he had made reparation of a sort and intercepted much that must have been intended her.

'At what are you laughing?'

'I was not laughing, my sister.'

'I saw your face in the moonlight. Why tell me a lie?'

'I am not lying.'

'Marcian! Marcian! Have you even after this warning no fear of eternal damnation?' She would have said more but was checked by the sound of hoofs. She was being pursued.

Marcian led the mule into the shadow of a rock, and Euric thundered past them. He looked magnificent suddenly, the torque sparkled, his face was set in a dream. Gallop of witch-craft and vengeance. He was calling to some fiend of the night. Twisted in the rocks, it sounded to Marcian like his own name.

She began to rejoice.

'Yes, sister, he has again missed you, and I know the path down into the plain, and there you will be safe. But sister, please refrain from singing. Your voice rings too sharp through the night and may lose you your virginity yet.'

She opened her mouth to rebuke him but fell silent. The re-appearance of the Goth had frightened her, and for the first time in her life she did as she was told. With bowed head, meditating on the universe whose earthly centre she supposed herself to be, she suffered her unworthy brother to guide her. He sought for patches of sand where the mule's feet fell softly, he extricated her chastity from the treacherous mountain curves, night light-ened, olives and vineyards crept around them at last, dawn would soon break over their father's farm, when Euric reap-peared, riding towards them, furiously.

Someone had to die this time and Marcian assumed it must be himself, and sprang into the middle of the path, ready to grapple, to be trampled on, he knew not what so long as it was his duty. But Euric swerved as they met, and bent sideways, and with both hands and terrific force crashed the torque round the boy's neck. 'Marcian!' he shouted, and this time the word rang clear. There was no doubt about it. He vanished into its echoes, leaving nothing behind him but a snake of dust.

Marcian picked himself up, bewildered. The torque fitted him and almost seemed part of him. He touched its rough-nesses and discovered that they were precious stones. Why had he been given it? And so skilfully? One of those stunning feats of horsemanship which were part of the barbarian legend. And were the Goths just warriors? Could they be warlocks as well?

He took hold of the mule and led it on, and they reached the farm without further adventure, and found there confusion of another sort. For some of the slaves in their retinue had found their way back during the night, and to cover their cowardice had spread tales of a great Gothic host which had carried the young master and mistress into captivity. Lucilla and the little girls were weeping, Justus was closeted with his bailiff to discuss the best method of ransom, the neighbours had been warned, the local legion, or what remained of it, was sending troops, and the Bishop had readily pronounced an anathema. And just as the confusion was at its height the sun rose, there were Marcian and Perpetua, she praising God as usual and he holding his head high and necklaced with gold.

Oh, then was sorrow turned into joy, as a resident catechist remarked, then was captivity led captive, and Marcian smothered in kisses. Perpetua declined any caress, for she now reserved herself for the Celestial Bridegroom, and it was not until she had changed her raiment and accepted refreshment that she consented to speak. She then related her adventures as she believed them to have occurred, and without the embellishments subsequently added to them by the Bishop. Her homily was dry and her sanctity so overwhelming that every word fell dead. 'And after that I had escaped from that Den of Lions,' she concluded, 'there was pursuit, but I erred as to its nature, for which no one can justly blame me. I supposed that that Son of Belial was renewing his assault, but his intention was otherwise. He pursued me to ask my pardon.'

'But how did you understand what he said, Perpetua?' interrupted one of the little girls. 'I did not know that Goths could speak.' She entertained extreme ideas about Goths.

'I should like to know what he said, however dreadful it was,' said the other little girl. 'Did he ask you to lie down?'

'Silence, Galla, silence, Justa,' their parents cried. 'Here are no matters for you.' But Perpetua responded not unbenignly. Looking at them and at Marcian against whom they were nestling, she explained the situation further: the Goth had not spoken, only meaningless shouts, but had done better than speech and offered all he possessed as a tribute to her virginity: he had given her that golden torque.

'He didn't,' cried Marcian before he could stop himself.

'He did, brother, and as an atonement for his sin. In the hope of escaping eternal punishment he cast it down at my feet.'

'He didn't. He cast it round my neck.'

She was too secure in her sanctity to take grave offence, and all that she said was, 'Brother, I am well aware of that. When I said he cast it down at my feet I spoke as David might have, poetically. It is sometimes permissible to be poetic and you would do well to study the Psalms more. Your Father Confessor shall be informed of this. He cast it round your neck because you were in attendance on me.'

'I wasn't.' The remark was childish, yet it caused his family to stir delightedly. It was the first time she had been gainsaid for years. She ignored him, clapped her hands, and ordered the slaves to place the torque in the basilica, where it would be dedicated to God. 'Father, are these your orders?' the boy cried.

Justus, still titular head of the house, looked annoyed. Lucilla ventured to say, 'Daughter; we know that the ornament is yours, but our son looks so manly in it, it so suits the cowing pride of his race. Daughter, could he not be allowed to display it up to the day of your own dedication?' She rejected this compromise and instructed the slaves to remove it by force. He was outraged and struggled and spat. 'It is mine,' he cried, 'he gave it me, and before the gods die I'll give something to him.' No one knew what he meant, and he did not yet know himself. 'Before the gods die' was a rustic oath which he ought not to have used. His parents smiled at hearing it on his lips, and it reminded them of older, easier days. 'Before the gods die I'll smack your bottom,' a peasant woman would say to her child. The torque kissed him goodbye as he blasphemed, and left upon each of his shoulders a small scarlet scar, which soon faded. Calm at once, he looked about him in a dazed fashion. 'What has happened?' he asked.

His sister then arranged for him to undergo a penance. The penances were not severe. It was their frequency that enfeebled.

During the five days before the dedication he became humble and helpful, busied himself on pious little errands and duly revered Perpetua. Their joint adventure grew dim, nothing confirmed it, and it might have faded away but for the Bishop's comparison of Euric to a horse. 'What about me?' he thought, and exploded with laughter. For he was not ill-equipped, the slave-girl had known as much four years ago. And he longed to meet the Goth in the hills again and bring him to his knees, and since that could not be he longed for the unholiness of night.

The night came, stormy and dark after the pageantry of the day. Everyone was tired, sanctity had not brought peace. The children were excited and had fits of screaming, and the old people disputed, which was rare. Justus feared that the torque might be stolen from the altar. Lucilla argued that no spirit, however evil, would go to such lengths. Marcian took his father's side, and undertook to set a guard. He then persuaded them to go to bed, went to his own chamber to find a cloak against the rain, and before he could put it on fell asleep.

He woke with a start, convinced that something had happened. As it had. He had forgotten to set the guard for the basilica, and if there had been a theft – the gods help him! He sprang up and went to inspect – it was only across the court-yard. The door was ajar, but when he looked in he could see, in the faint light of candles, that nothing had been disturbed. The torque stood in its usual position.

But lovelier than usual. He had forgotten how large it was, how it glowed and curved like a snake, how its roughnesses intoxicated. He was alone with it at last and for the last time. It had been round his lover's neck once. The recollection made him go all faint. He swayed against it and found himself in his lover's arms. And he knew, without being told, that Euric, Euric the trickster, had lurked about the farm all day and hidden in the shadows to take him just like this, and he prepared to meet his former fate.

But things did not go as before. Euric was somehow different. He missed opportunities and failed to strike, and presently with an impatient grunt he flung himself face downwards on the basilica floor. The caprices of the barbarians are infinite, and this time he wanted to be raped.

Well, he should be and it wouldn't take long. The boy flung his garment off and mounted. Heaven opened and he rode like a devil, his head down, his heels in the air. *Itque reditque viam totiens*,[4] as a pagan poet puts it, *destillat ab inguine virus*,[5] and as it did so they fused. They had fused into a single monster such as trouble the vigils of saints. He would have withdrawn now but it was too late. Clamped by his lust, he was already half Goth, he felt heavings of laughter which became his own, they could talk without speaking, they never stopped loving, and presently they started to fly. They flew round and round the basilica and defiled it, they shot through its roof into the storm-torn night. There was a blinding lightning flash, and for one delirious moment he saw the farmyard beneath him and all the animals looking up. Then he fell through his own ceiling into his bed and awoke.

It had been a dream, and one for which he would have to do penance. But a dream so violent and warm that it must have been shared.

He sat up and reflected. After all, Goths do sometimes fly. That much is common knowledge. Only last year one of them had haled up an old woman who was hoeing turnips and dropped her into a muck-heap. They cannot fly far – the inscrutable decrees of Providence prevent them. Still, the basilica could not be called far. He got out of his bed to look at it and so discovered that it was on fire.

The alarm had already been given. Slaves shouted, children screamed, a monk pulled a bell, his mother had been hit by the bough of a falling tree. A tempest was abroad, alternating thunder with spouts of rain, and someone had unfastened the gate of the farmyard, and the horses had got out and were going wild. He found his father and they tried to establish order. The basilica, they noted, was not exactly burning, it was flickering with intense luminosity. What really mattered was the increasing panic, which they had not the skill to control.

It was stilled by the arrival of Perpetua.

Clad all in white, she issued from her apartment, advanced majestically and said, 'My people, what is amiss?' It was the first time she had called everyone her people. And when she saw the quivering basilica she exclaimed: 'It is the Enemy, it is the unhallowed one. By what means he entered I know not, but I will destroy him.'

'Save us,' all the people cried.

'With God's help I will do so.'

It was at this point that Marcian flung himself across her path and said, 'Sister, desist.' She heard him but did not reply. He was beneath her attention. 'Sister, do not, oh I implore you do not,' he went on. 'I do not, I cannot speak but oh keep away from the place. It may be that seeds of devils – it cannot be, but do not risk it. I think I dreamed, yet I may dream that I dreamt, in which case the white-hot droppings – ' As he said this the basilica's doors opened, and far within on the altar the torque showed scarlet. He cried: 'Yes, there he is, there. We have been from him once – that is to say, you have and I do not signify. Let me save you again.'

She paid no heed to such childishness, but his last words annoyed her, and she permitted herself to say scornfully, 'Save me, brother? You save *me*?' and went out intrepidly into the storm. There was a miraculous lull, and all could see her in the plenitude of her sanctitude and power. *Virgo victrix*, she continued to advance. She entered the basilica, and as she did so a thunderbolt fell and reduced it and her to ashes.

It was the end of the world, or so they all thought, and so the Bishop thought as soon as the state of the roads permitted him to return and investigate. He had always been suspicious of this farm and its inmates and now he ordered exorcism, but it came too late. There was nothing to exorcise. The place seemed equally dispossessed of good and of evil. He departed disconsolate, and a number of the religious followed him, leaving a spiritual void.

Only the animals remained unaffected by the catastrophe. They clucked and copulated as usual. And the fields revived after the rain and promised bumper crops. Marcian had to see to this. There was so much work to do that he had not the time to repent. He duly recognised in his spare moments that his impiety and lechery were to blame and might damn him eternally, and he duly mourned his distinguished sister and collected what could be found of her into an urn. But what a relief not to have her about! And what an economy to be free of her hangers-on! A few hermits remained, a few shrines of an earlier religion returned, no one disputed, no one denounced, and the farm began to prosper. Fortunately it lay out of the route of the barbarian invasions that devastated the rest of the province. It became a charmed spot, and became gay and happy as well as energetic, and no longer yearned nostalgically for the hills. Home sweet home was enough. His parents adored him, and he procured them a comfortable and amusing old age. His little sisters adored him, and in due time he took their virginities. He never saw Euric again but could always send him messages – any young Goth would accept one. And he gave the name of Euric to his favourite mare, whose stable he shared on dark nights, and upon whom at the heroic moment he could be seen thundering across the sky, clamped, necklaced in gold.

The Other Boat

I

'Cocoanut, come and play at soldiers.'

'I cannot, I am beesy.'

'But you must, Lion wants you.'

'Yes, come along, man,' said Lionel, running up with some paper cocked hats and a sash. It was long long ago, and little boys still went to their deaths stiffly, and dressed in as many clothes as they could find.

'I cannot, I am beesy,' repeated Cocoanut.

'But man, what are you busy about?'

'I have soh many things to arrange, man.'

'Let's leave him and play by ourselves,' said Olive. 'We've Joan and Noel and Baby and Lieutenant Bodkin. Who wants Cocoanut?'

'Oh, shut up! *I* want him. We must have him. He's the only one who falls down when he's killed. All you others go on fighting long too long. The battle this morning was a perfect fast. Mother said so.'

'Well, I'll die.'

'So you say beforehand, but when it comes to the point you won't. Noel won't. Joan won't. Baby doesn't do anything properly – of course he's too little – and you can't expect Lieutenant Bodkin to fall down. Cocoanut, man, do.'

'I – weel – not.'

'Cocoanut cocoanut cocoanut cocoanut cocoanut cocoanut,' said Baby.

The little boy rolled on the deck screaming happily. He liked to be pressed by these handsome good-natured children. 'I must go and see the m'm m'm m'm,' he said.

'The what?'

'The m'm m'm m'm. They live – oh, so many of them – in the thin part of the ship.'

'He means in the bow,' said Olive. 'Oh, come along, Lion. He's hopeless.'

'What are m'm m'm m'm?'

'M'm.' He whirled his arms about, and chalked some marks on the planks.

'What are those?'

'M'm.'

'What's their name?'

'They have no name.'

'What do they do?'

'They just go so and oh! and so – ever – always – '

'Flying fish?… Fairies?… Noughts and crosses?'

'They have no name.'

'Mother!' said Olive to a lady who was promenading with a gentleman, 'hasn't everything a name?'

'I suppose so.'

'Who's this?' asked the lady's companion.

'He's always hanging on to my children. I don't know.'

'Touch of the tar-brush, eh?'

'Yes, but it doesn't matter on a voyage home. I would never allow it going to India.' They passed on, Mrs March calling back, 'Shout as much as you like, boys, but don't scream, don't scream.'

'They must have a name,' said Lionel, recollecting, 'because Adam named all the animals when the Bible was beginning.'

'They weren't in the Bible, m'm m'm m'm; they were all the time up in the thin part of the sheep, and when you pop out they pop in, so how could Adam have?'

'Noah's ark is what he's got to now.'

Baby said, 'Noah's ark, Noah's ark, Noah's ark,' and they all bounced up and down and roared. Then, without any compact, they drifted from the saloon deck on to the lower, and from the lower down the staircase that led to the castle, much as the weeds and jellies were drifting about outside in the tropical sea. Soldiering was forgotten, though Lionel said, 'We may as well wear our cocked hats.' They played with a fox terrier, who was in the charge of a sailor, and asked the sailor himself if a roving life was a happy one. Then, drifting forward again, they climbed into the bows, where the m'm m'm m'm were said to be.

Here opened a glorious country, much the best in the boat. None of the March children had explored there before, but Cocoanut, having few domesticities, knew it well. That bell that hung in the very peak – it was the ship's bell and if you rang it the ship would stop. Those big ropes were tied into knots – twelve knots an hour. This paint was wet, but only as far as there. Up that hole was coming a Lascar. But of the m'm m'm he said nothing until asked. Then he explained in offhand tones that if you popped out they popped in, so that you couldn't expect to see them.

What treachery! How disappointing! Yet so ill-balanced were the children's minds that they never complained. Olive, in whom the instincts of a lady were already awaking, might have said a few well-chosen words, but when she saw her brothers happy she forgot too, and lifted Baby up on to a bollard because he asked her to. They all screamed. Into their midst came the Lascar and laid down a mat for his three-o'clock prayer. He prayed as if he was still in India, facing westward, not knowing that the ship had rounded Arabia so that his holy places now lay behind him. They continued to scream.

Mrs March and her escort remained on the saloon deck, inspecting the approach to Suez. Two continents were converging with great magnificence of mountains and plain. At their junction, nobly placed, could be seen the smoke and the trees of the town. In addition to her more personal problems, she had become anxious about Pharaoh. 'Where exactly was

Pharaoh drowned?' she asked Captain Armstrong. 'I shall have to show my boys.' Captain Armstrong did not know, but he offered to ask Mr Hotblack, the Moravian missionary. Mr Hotblack knew – in fact he knew too much. Somewhat snubbed by the military element in the earlier part of the voyage, he now bounced to the surface, became authoritative and officious, and undertook to wake Mrs March's little ones when they were passing the exact spot. He spoke of the origins of Christianity in a way that made her look down her nose, saying that the Canal was one long genuine Bible picture gallery, that donkeys could still be seen going down into Egypt carrying Holy Families, and naked Arabs wading into the water to fish; 'Peter and Andrew by Galilee's shore, why, it hits the truth plumb.' A clergyman's daughter and a soldier's wife, she could not admit that Christianity had ever been oriental. What good thing can come out of the Levant, and is it likely that the apostles ever had a touch of the tar-brush? Still, she thanked Mr Hotblack (for, having asked a favour of him, she had contracted an obligation towards him), and she resigned herself to greeting him daily until Southampton, when their paths would part.

Then she observed, against the advancing land, her children playing in the bows without their topis on. The sun in those far-off days was a mighty power and hostile to the Ruling Race. Officers staggered at a touch of it, Tommies collapsed. When the regiment was under canvas, it wore helmets at tiffin, lest the rays penetrated the tent. She shouted at her doomed offspring, she gesticulated, Captain Armstrong and Mr Hotblack shouted, but the wind blew their cries backwards. Refusing company, she hurried forward alone; the children were far too excited and covered with paint.

'Lionel! Olive! Olive! What are you doing?'

'M'm m'm m'm, mummy – it's a new game.'

'Go back and play properly under the awning at once – it's far too hot. You'll have sunstroke every one of you. Come, Baby!'

'M'm m'm m'm.'

'Now, you won't want me to carry a great boy like you, surely.'

Baby flung himself round the bollard and burst into tears.

'It always ends like this,' said Mrs March as she detached him. 'You all behave foolishly and selfishly and then Baby cries. No, Olive – don't help me. Mother would rather do everything herself.'

'Sorry,' said Lionel gruffly. Baby's shrieks rent the air. Thoroughly naughty, he remained clasping an invisible bollard. As she bent him into a portable shape, another mishap occurred. A sailor – an Englishman – leapt out of the hatchway with a piece of chalk and drew a little circle round her where she stood. Cocoanut screamed, 'He's caught you. He's come.'

'You're on dangerous ground, lady,' said the sailor respectfully. 'Men's quarters. Of course we leave it to your generosity.'

Tired with the voyage and the noise of the children, worried by what she had left in India and might find in England, Mrs March fell into a sort of trance. She stared at the circle stupidly, unable to move out of it, while Cocoanut danced round her and gibbered.

'Men's quarters – just to keep up the old custom.'

'I don't understand.'

'Passengers are often kind enough to pay their footing,' he said, feeling awkward; though rapacious he was independent. 'But of course there's no compulsion, lady. Ladies and gentlemen do as they feel.'

'I will certainly do what is customary – Baby, *be* quiet.'

'Thank you, lady. We divide whatever you give among the crew. Of course not those chaps.' He indicated the Lascar.

'The money shall be sent to you. I have no purse.'

He touched his forelock cynically. He did not believe her. She stepped out of the circle and as she did so Cocoanut sprang into it and squatted grinning.

'You're a silly little boy and I shall complain to the stewardess about you,' she told him with unusual heat. 'You never will play any game properly and you stop the others. You're a silly, idle, useless, unmanly little boy.'

2

S.S. Normannia
Red Sea
October, 191–

Hullo the Mater!

You may be thinking it is about time I wrote you a line, so here goes, however you should have got my wire sent before leaving Tilbury with the glad news that I got a last minute passage on this boat when it seemed quite impossible I should do so. The Arbuthnots are on it too all right, so is a Lady Manning who claims acquaintance with Olive, not to mention several remarkably cheery subalterns, poor devils, don't know what they are in for in the tropics. We make up two Bridge tables every night besides hanging together at other times, and get called the Big Eight, which I suppose must be regarded as a compliment. How I got my passage is curious. I was coming away from the S.S. office after my final try in absolute despair when I ran into an individual whom you may or may not remember – he was a kid on that other boat when we cleared all out of India on that unlikely occasion over ten years ago –

got called Cocoanut because of his peculiar shaped head. He has now turned into an equally weird youth, who has however managed to become influential in shipping circles. I can't think how some people manage to do things. He duly recognised me – dagoes sometimes have marvellous memories – and on learning my sad plight fixed me up with a (single berth) cabin, so all is well. He is on board too, but our paths seldom cross. He has more than a touch of the tar-brush, so consorts with his own dusky fraternity, no doubt to their mutual satisfaction.

The heat is awful and I fear this is but a dull letter in consequence. Bridge I have already mentioned, and there are the usual deck games, betting on the ship's log, etc., still I think everyone will be glad to reach Bombay and get into harness. Colonel and Mrs Arbuthnot are very friendly, and speaking confidentially I don't think it will do my prospects any harm having got to know them better. Well I will now conclude this screed and I will write again when I have rejoined the regiment and contacted Isabel. Best love to all which naturally includes yourself from

Your affectionate first born
Lionel March.

P.S. Lady Manning asks to be remembered to Olive, nearly forgot.

When Captain March had posted this epistle he rejoined the Big Eight. Although he had spent the entire day with them they were happy to see him, for he exactly suited them. He was what any rising young officer ought to be – clean-cut, athletic, good-looking without being conspicuous. He had had wonderful professional luck, which no one grudged him: he had got into one of the little desert wars that were becoming too rare, had displayed dash and decision, had been wounded, and had been mentioned in despatches and got his captaincy early. Success had not spoiled him, nor was he vain of his personal appearance, although he must have known that thick fairish hair, blue eyes, glowing cheeks and strong white teeth constitute, when broad shoulders support them, a combination irresistible to the fair sex. His hands were clumsier than the rest of him, but bespoke hard honest work, and the springy gleaming hairs on them suggested virility. His voice was quiet, his demeanour assured, his temper equable. Like his brother officers he wore a mess uniform slightly too small for him, which accentuated his physique – the ladies accentuating theirs by wearing their second best frocks and reserving their best ones for India.

Bridge proceeded without a hitch, as his mother had been given to understand it might. She had not been told that on either side of the players, violet darkening into black, rushed the sea, nor would she have been interested. Her son gazed at it occasionally, his forehead furrowed. For despite his outstanding advantages he was a miserable cardplayer, and he was having wretched luck. As soon as the *Normannia* entered the Mediterranean he had begun to lose, and the 'better luck after Port Said, always the case' that had been humorously promised him had never arrived. Here in the Red Sea he had lost the maximum the Big Eight's moderate stakes allowed. He couldn't afford it, he had no private means and he ought to be saving up for the future, also it was humiliating to let down his partner: Lady Manning herself. So he was thankful when play terminated and the usual drinks circulated. They sipped and gulped while the lighthouses on the Arabian coast winked at them and slid northwards. 'Bedfordshire' fell pregnantly from the lips of Mrs Arbuthnot. And they dispersed, with the certainty that the day which was approaching would exactly resemble the one that had died.

In this they were wrong.

Captain March waited until all was quiet, still frowning at the sea. Then with something alert and predatory about him, something disturbing and disturbed, he went down to his cabin.

'Come een,' said a sing-song voice.

For it was not a single cabin, as he had given his mother to understand. There were two berths, and the lower one contained Cocoanut. Who was naked. A brightly coloured scarf lay across him and contrasted with his blackish-greyish skin, and an aromatic smell came off him, not at all unpleasant. In ten years he had developed into a personable adolescent, but still had the same funny-shaped head. He had been doing his accounts and now he laid them down and gazed at the British officer adoringly.

'Man, I thought you was never coming,' he said, and his eyes filled with tears.

'It's only those bloody Arbuthnots and their blasted bridge,' replied Lionel and closed the cabin door.

'I thought you was dead.'

'Well, I'm not.'

'I thought I should die.'

'So you will.' He sat down on the berth, heavily and with deliberate heaviness. The end of the chase was in sight. It had not been a long one. He had always liked the kid, even on that other boat, and now he liked him more than ever. Champagne in an ice bucket too. An excellent kid. They couldn't associate on deck with that touch of the tar-brush, but it was a very different business down here, or soon would be. Lowering his voice, he said, 'The trouble is we're not supposed to do this sort of thing under any circumstances whatsoever, which you never seem to understand. If we got caught there'd be absolute bloody hell to pay, yourself as well as me, so for God's sake don't make a noise.'

'Lionel, O Lion of the Night, love me.'

'All right. Stay where you are.' Then he confronted the magic that had been worrying him on and off the whole evening and had made him inattentive at cards. A tang of sweat spread as he stripped and a muscle thickened up out of gold. When he was ready he shook off old Cocoanut, who was now climbing about like a monkey, and put him where he had to be, and manhandled him, gently, for he feared his own strength and was always gentle, and closed on him, and they did what they both wanted to do.

Wonderful, wonnerful...

They lay entwined, Nordic warrior and subtle supple boy, who belonged to no race and always got what he wanted. All his life he had wanted a toy that would not break, and now he was planning how he would play with Lionel for ever. He had longed for him ever since their first meeting, embraced him in dreams when only that was possible, met him again as the omens foretold, and marked him down, spent money to catch him and lime him, and here he lay, caught, and did not know it.

There they lay caught, both of them, and did not know it, while the ship carried them inexorably towards Bombay.

3

It had not always been so wonderful, wonnerful. Indeed the start of the affair had been grotesque and nearly catastrophic. Lionel had stepped on board at Tilbury entirely the simple soldier man, without an inkling of his fate. He had thought it decent of a youth whom he had only known as a child to fix him up with a cabin, but had not expected to find the fellow on board too – still less to have to share the cabin with him. This gave him a nasty shock. British officers are never stabled with dagoes, never, it was too damn awkward for words. However, he could not very well protest under the circumstances, nor did he in his heart want to, for his colour-prejudices were tribal rather than personal, and only worked when an observer was present. The first half-hour together went most pleasantly, they were unpacking and sorting things out before the ship started, he found his childhood's acquaintance friendly and quaint, exchanged reminiscences, and even started teasing and bossing him as in the old days, and got him giggling delightedly. He sprang up to his berth and sat on its edge, swinging his legs. A hand touched them, and he thought no harm until it approached their junction. Then he became puzzled, scared and disgusted in quick succession, leapt down with a coarse barrackroom oath and a brow of thunder and went straight to the Master at Arms to report an offence against decency. Here he showed the dash and decision that had so advantaged him in desert warfare: in other words he did not know what he was doing.

The Master at Arms could not be found, and during the delay Lionel's rage abated somewhat, and he reflected that if he lodged a formal complaint he would have to prove it, which he could not do, and might have to answer questions, at which he was never good. So he went to the Purser instead, and he demanded to be given alternative accommodation, without stating any reason for the change. The Purser stared: the boat was chockablock full already, as Captain March must have known. 'Don't speak to me like that,' Lionel stormed, and shouldered his way to the gunwale to see England recede. Here was the worst thing in the world, the thing for which Tommies got given the maximum, and here was he bottled up with it for a fortnight. What the hell was he to do? Go forward with the charge or blow his own brains out or what?

On to him thus desperately situated the Arbuthnots descended. They were slight acquaintances, their presence calmed him, and before long his light military guffaw rang out as if nothing had happened. They were pleased to see him, for they were hurriedly forming a group of sahibs who would hang together during the voyage and exclude outsiders. With his help the Big Eight came into being, soon to be the envy of less happy passengers; introductions; drinks; jokes; difficulties of securing a berth. At this point Lionel made a shrewd move: everything gets known on a boat and he had better anticipate discovery. 'I got a passage all right,' he brayed, 'but at the cost of sharing my cabin with a wog.' All condoled, and Colonel Arbuthnot in the merriest of moods exclaimed, 'Let's hope the blacks don't come off on the sheets,' and Mrs Arbuthnot, wittier still, cried, 'Of course they won't, dear, if it's a wog it'll be the coffees.' Everyone shouted with laughter, the good lady basked in the applause, and Lionel could not understand why he suddenly wanted to throw himself into the sea. It was so unfair, he was the aggrieved party, yet he felt himself in the wrong and almost a cad. If only he had found out the fellow's tastes in England he would never have touched him, no, not with tongs. But could he have found out? You couldn't tell by just looking. Or could you? Dimly, after ten years' forgetfulness, something stirred in that faraway boat of his childhood and he saw his mother... Well, she was always objecting to something or other, the poor Mater. No, he couldn't possibly have known.

The Big Eight promptly reserved tables for lunch and all future meals, and Cocoanut and his set were relegated to a second sitting – for it became evident that he too was in a set: the tagrag and coloured bobtail stuff that accumulates in corners and titters and whispers, and may well be influential, but who cares? Lionel regarded it with distaste and looked for a touch of the hangdog in his unspeakable cabin-mate, but he was skipping and gibbering on the promenade deck as if nothing had occurred. He himself was safe for the moment, eating curry by the side of Lady Manning, and amusing her by his joke about the various names which the cook would give the same curry on successive days. Again something stabbed him and he thought: 'But what shall I do, *do*, when night comes? There will have to be some sort of showdown.' After lunch the weather deteriorated. England said farewell to her children with her choppiest seas, her gustiest winds, and the banging of invisible pots and pans in the empyrean. Lady Manning thought she might do better in a deckchair. He squired her to it and then collapsed and re-entered his cabin as rapidly as he had left it a couple of hours earlier.

It now seemed full of darkies, who rose to their feet as he retched, assisted him up to his berth and loosened his collar, after which the gong summoned them to their lunch. Presently Cocoanut and his elderly Parsee secretary looked in to inquire and were civil and helpful and he could not but thank them. The showdown must be postponed. Later in the day he felt better and less inclined for it, and the night did not bring its dreaded perils or indeed anything at all. It was almost as if nothing had happened – almost but not quite. Master Cocoanut had learned his lesson, for he pestered no more, yet he skilfully implied that the lesson was an unimportant one. He was like someone who has been refused a loan and indicates that he will not apply again. He seemed positively not to mind his disgrace – incomprehensibly to Lionel, who expected either repentance or terror. Could it be that he himself had made too much fuss?

In this uneventful atmosphere the voyage across the Bay of Biscay proceeded. It was clear that his favours would not again be asked, and he could not help wondering what would have happened if he had granted them. Propriety was re-established, almost monotonously; if he and Cocoanut overlapped in the cabin and had to settle (for instance) who should wash first, they solved the problem with mutual tact.

And then the ship entered the Mediterranean.

Resistance weakened under the balmier sky, curiosity increased. It was an exquisite afternoon – their first decent weather. Cocoanut was leaning out of the porthole to see the sunlit rock of Gibraltar. Lionel leant against him to look too and permitted a slight, a very slight familiarity with his person. The ship did not sink nor did the heavens fall. The contact started something whirling about inside his head and all over him, he could not concentrate on after-dinner bridge, he felt excited, frightened and powerful all at once and kept looking at the stars. Cocoa, who said weird things sometimes, declared that the stars were moving into a good place and could be kept there.

That night champagne appeared in the cabin, and he was seduced. He never could resist champagne. Curse, oh curse! How on earth had it happened? Never again. More happened off the coast of Sicily, more, much more at Port Said, and here in the Red Sea they slept together as a matter of course.

4

And this particular night they lay motionless for longer than usual, as though something in the fall of their bodies had enchanted them. They had never been so content with each other before, and only one of them realised that nothing lasts, that they might be more happy or less happy in the future, but would never again be exactly thus. He tried not to stir, not to breathe, not to live even, but life was too strong for him and he sighed.

'All right?' whispered Lionel.

'Yes.'

'Did I hurt?'

'Yes.'

'Sorry.'

'Why?'

'Can I have a drink?'

'You can have the whole world.'

'Lie still and I'll get you one too, not that you deserve it after making such a noise.'

'Was I again a noise?'

'You were indeed. Never mind, you shall have a nice drink.' Half Ganymede, half Goth, he jerked a bottle out of the ice-bucket. Pop went a cork and hit the partition wall. Sounds of feminine protest became audible, and they both laughed. 'Here, hurry up, scuttle up and drink.' He offered the goblet, received it back, drained it, refilled. His eyes shone, any depths through which he might have passed were forgotten. 'Let's make a night of it,' he suggested. For he was of the conventional type who once the conventions are broken breaks them into little pieces, and for an hour or two there was nothing he wouldn't say or do.

Meanwhile the other one, the deep one, watched. To him the moment of ecstasy was sometimes the moment of vision, and his cry of delight when they closed had wavered into fear. The fear passed before he could understand what it meant or against what it warned him, against nothing perhaps. Still, it seemed wiser to watch. As in business, so in love, precautions are desirable, insurances must be effected. 'Man, shall we now perhaps have our cigarette?' he asked.

This was an established ritual, an assertion deeper than speech that they belonged to each other and in their own way. Lionel assented and lit the thing, pushed it between dusky lips, pulled it out, pulled at it, replaced it, and they smoked it alternately with their faces touching. When it was finished Cocoa refused to extinguish the butt in an ashtray but consigned it through the porthole into the flying waters with incomprehensible words. He thought the words might protect them, though he could not explain how, or what they were.

'That reminds me...' said Lionel, and stopped. He had been reminded, and for no reason, of his mother. He did not want to mention her in his present state, the poor old Mater, especially after all the lies she had been told.

'Yes, what did it remind you, our cigarette? Yes and please? I should know.'

'Nothing.' And he stretched himself, flawless except for a scar down in the groin.

'Who gave you that?'

'One of your fuzzy-wuzzy cousins.'

'Does it hurt?'

'No.' It was a trophy from the little desert war. An assegai had nearly unmanned him, nearly but not quite, which Cocoa said was a good thing. A dervish, a very holy man told him that what nearly destroys may bring strength and can be summoned in the hour of revenge. 'I've no use for revenge,' Lionel said.

'Oh Lion, why not when it can be so sweet?'

He shook his head and reached up for his pyjamas, a sultan's gift. It was presents all the time in these days. His gambling debts were settled through the secretary, and if he needed anything, or was thought to need it, something or other appeared. He had ceased to protest and now accepted indiscriminately. He could trade away the worst of the junk later on – some impossible jewellery for instance which one couldn't be seen dead in. He did wish, though, that he could have given presents in return, for he was anything but a sponger. He had made an attempt two nights previously, with dubious results. 'I seem always taking and never giving,' he had said. 'Is there nothing of mine you'd fancy? I'd be so glad if there was.' To receive the reply: 'Yes. Your hairbrush' – 'My *hairbrush*?' – and he was not keen on parting with this particular object, for it had been a coming-of-age gift from Isabel. His hesitation brought tears to the eyes, so he had to give in. 'You're welcome to my humble brush if you want it, of course. I'll just comb it out for you first' – 'No, no, as it is, uncombed,' and it was snatched away fanatically. Almost like a vulture snatching. Odd little things like this did happen occasionally, m'm m'm m'ms he called them, for they reminded him of oddities on the other boat. They did no one any harm, so why worry? Enjoy yourself while you can. He lolled at his ease and let the gifts rain on him as they would – a Viking at a Byzantine court, spoiled, adored and not yet bored.

This was certainly the life, and sitting on one chair with his feet on another he prepared for their usual talk, which might be long or short but was certainly the life. When Cocoanut got going it was fascinating. For all the day he had slipped around the ship, discovering people's weaknesses. More than that, he and his cronies were cognisant of financial possibilities that do not appear in the City columns, and could teach one how to get rich if one thought it worth while. More than that, he had a vein of fantasy. In the midst of something ribald and scandalous – the discovery of Lady Manning, for instance: Lady Manning of all people in the cabin of the Second Engineer – he imagined the discovery being made by a flying fish who had popped through the Engineer's porthole, and he indicated the expression on the fish's face.

Yes, this was the life, and one that he had never experienced in his austere apprenticeship: luxury, gaiety, kindness, unusualness, and delicacy that did not exclude brutal pleasure. Hitherto he had been ashamed of being built like a brute: his preceptors had condemned carnality or had dismissed it as a waste of time, and his mother had ignored its existence in him and all her children; being hers, they had been pure.

What to talk about this pleasurable evening? How about the passport scandal? For Cocoanut possessed two passports, not one like most people, and they confirmed a growing suspicion that he might not be altogether straight. In England Lionel would have sheered off at once from such a subject, but since Gibraltar they had become so intimate and morally relaxed that he experienced nothing but friendly curiosity. The information on the passports was conflicting, so that it was impossible to tell the twister's age, or where he had been born or indeed what his name was. 'You could get into serious trouble over this,' Lionel had warned him, to be answered by irresponsible giggles. 'You could, you know. However, you're no better than a monkey, and I suppose a monkey can't be expected to know its own name.' To which the reply had been 'Lion, he don't know nothing at all. Monkey's got to come along to tell a Lion he's alive.' It was never easy to score. He had picked up his education, if that was the word for it, in London, and his financial beginnings in Amsterdam, one of the passports was Portuguese, the other Danish, and half the blood must be Asiatic, unless a drop was Negro.

'Now come along, tell me the truth and nothing but the truth for a change,' he began. 'Ah, that reminds me I've at last got off that letter to the Mater. She adores news. It was a bit difficult to think of anything to interest her, however I filled it up with tripe about the Arbuthnots, and threw you in at the end as a sort of makeweight.'

'To make what sort of weight?'

'Well, naturally I didn't say what we do. I'm not stark staring raving mad. I merely mentioned I'd run into you in the London office, and got a cabin through you, that is to say a single-berth one. I threw dust in her eyes all right.'

'Dear Lionel, you don't know how to throw dust or even where it is. Of mud you know a little, good, but not dust. Why bring me into the matter at all?'

'For the sake of something to say.'

'Did you say I too was on board?'

'I did in passing,' he said irritably, for he now realised he had better not have. 'I was writing that damned epistle, not you, and I had to fill it up. Don't worry – she's forgotten your very existence by this time.'

The other was certain she hadn't. If he had foreseen this meeting and had worked towards it through dreams, why should not an anxious parent have foreseen it too? She had reasons for anxiety, for things had actually started on that other boat. A trivial collision between children had alerted them towards each other as men. Thence had their present happiness sprung, thither might it wither, for the children had been disturbed. That vengeful onswishing of skirts... 'What trick can I think of this time that will keep him from her? I love him, I am clever, I have money. I will try.' The first step was to contrive his exit from the Army. The second step was to dispose of that English girl in India, called Isabel, about whom too little was known. Marriage or virginity or concubinage for Isabel? He had no scruples at perverting Lionel's instincts in order to gratify his own, or at endangering his prospects of paternity. All that mattered was their happiness, and he thought he knew what that was. Much depended on the next few days: he had to work hard and to work with the stars. His mind played round approaching problems, combining them, retreating from them, and aware all the time of a further problem, of something in the beloved which he did not understand. He half-closed his eyes and watched, and listened through half-closed ears. By not being too much on the spot and sacrificing shrewdness to vision he sometimes opened a door. And sure enough Lionel said, 'As a matter of fact the Mater never liked you,' and a door opened, slowly.

'Man, how should she? Oh, when the chalk went from the hand of the sailor round the feet of the lady and she could not move and we all knew it, and oh man how we mocked her.'

'I don't remember – well, I do a little. It begins to come back to me and does sound like the sort of thing that would put her off. She certainly went on about you after we landed, and complained that you made things interesting when they weren't, funny thing to say, still the Mater is pretty funny. So we put our heads together as children sometimes do – '

'Do they? Oh yes.'

' – and Olive who's pretty bossy herself decreed we wouldn't mention you again as it seemed to worry her extra and she had just had a lot of worry. He actually – I hadn't meant to tell you this, it's a dead secret.'

'It shall be. I swear. By all that is without me and within me I swear.' He became incomprehensible in his excitement and uttered words in that unknown tongue. Nearly all tongues were unknown to Lionel, and he was impressed.

'Well, he actually – '

'Man, of whom do you now speak?'

'Oh yes, the Mater's husband, my Dad. He was in the Army too, in fact he attained the rank of major, but a quite unspeakable thing happened – he went native somewhere out East and got cashiered – deserted his wife and left her with five young children to bring up, and no money. She was taking us all away from him when you met us and still had a faint hope that he might pull himself together and follow her. Not he. He never even wrote – remember, this is absolutely secret.'

'Yes, yes,' but he thought the secret a very tame one: how else should a middle-aged husband behave? 'But, Lionel, one question to you the more. For whom did the Major desert the Mater?'

'He went native.'

'With a girl or with a boy?'

'A boy? Good God! Well, I mean to say, with a girl, naturally – I mean, it was somewhere right away in the depths of Burma.'

'Even in Burma there are boys. At least I once heard so. But the Dad went native with a girl. Ver' well. Might not therefore there be offspring?'

'If there were, they'd be half-castes. Pretty depressing prospect. Well, you know what I mean. My family – Dad's, that's to say – can trace itself back nearly two hundred years, and the Mater's goes back to the War of the Roses. It's really pretty awful, Cocoa.'

The half-caste smiled as the warrior floundered. Indeed he valued him most when he fell full length. And the whole conversation – so unimportant in itself – gave him a sense of approaching victory which he had not so far entertained. He had a feeling that Lionel knew that he was in the net or almost in it, and did not mind. Cross-question him further! Quick! Rattle him! 'Is Dad dead?' he snapped.

'I couldn't very well come East if he wasn't. He has made our name stink in these parts. As it is I've had to change my name, or rather drop half of it. He called himself Major Corrie March. We were all proud of the "Corrie" and had a reason to be. Try saying "Corrie March" to the Big Eight here, and watch the effect.'

'You must get two passports, must you not, one with and one without a "Corrie" on it. I will fix it, yes? At Bombay?'

'So as I can cheat like you? No, thank you. My name is Lionel March and that's my name.' He poured out some more champagne.

'Are you like him?'

'I should hope not. I hope I'm not cruel and remorseless and selfish and self-indulgent and a liar as he was.'

'I don't mean unimportant things like that. I mean are you like him to look at?'

'You have the strangest ideas of what is important.'

'Was his body like yours?'

'How should I know?' – and he was suddenly shy. 'I was only a kid and the Mater's torn up every photograph of him she could lay her hands on. He was a hundred per cent Aryan all right, and there was plenty of him as there certainly is of me – indeed there'll be too much of me if I continue swilling at this rate. Suppose we talk about passports for a change.'

'Was he one in whom those who sought rest found fire, and fire rest?'

'I've not the least idea what you're talking about. Do you mean I'm such a one myself?'

'I do.'

'I've not the least idea – ' Then he hesitated. 'Unless... no, you're daft as usual, and in any case we've spent more than enough time in dissecting my unfortunate parent. I brought him up to show you how much the Mater has to put up with, one has to make endless allowances for her and you mustn't take it amiss if she's unreasonable about you. She'd probably like you if she got the chance. There was something else that upset her at the time... I seem to be bringing out all the family skeletons in a bunch, still they won't go any further, and I feel like chattering to someone about everything, once in a way. I've never had anyone to talk to like you. Never, and don't suppose I ever shall. Do you happen to remember the youngest of us all, the one we called Baby?'

'Ah, that pretty Baby!'

'Well, a fortnight after we landed and while we were up at my grandfather's looking for a house, that poor kid died.'

'Die what of?' he exclaimed, suddenly agitated. He raised his knees and rested his chin on them. With his nudity and his polished duskiness and his strange-shaped head, he suggested an image crouched outside a tomb.

'Influenza, quite straightforward. It was going through the parish and he caught it. But the worst of it was the Mater wouldn't be reasonable. She would insist that it was sunstroke, and that he got it running about with no topi on when she wasn't looking after him properly in this very same Red Sea.'

'Her poor pretty Baby. So I killed him for her.'

'Cocoa! However did you guess that? It's exactly what she twisted it round to. We had quite a time with her. Olive argued, grandfather prayed… and I could only hang around and do the wrong thing, as I generally do.'

'But she – she saw me only, running in the sun with my devil's head, and m'm m'm m'm all you follow me till the last one the tiny one dies, and she, she talking to an officer, a handsome one, oh to sleep in his arms as I shall in yours, so she forgets the sun and it strikes the tiny one. I see.'

'Yes, you see in a wrong sort of way'; every now and then came these outbursts which ought to be rubbish yet weren't. Wrong of course about his mother, who was the very soul of purity, and over Captain Armstrong, who had become their valued family adviser. But right over Baby's death: she actually had declared that the idle unmanly imp had killed him, and designedly. Of recent years she had not referred to the disaster and might have forgotten it. He was more than ever vexed with himself for mentioning Cocoanut in the letter he had recently posted to her.

'Did I kill him for you also?'

'For me? Of course not. I know the difference between influenza and sunstroke, and you don't develop the last-named after a three weeks' interval.'

'Did I kill him for anyone – or for anything?'

Lionel gazed into eyes that gazed through him and through cabin walls into the sea. A few days ago he would have ridiculed the question, but tonight he was respectful. This was because his affection, having struck earthward, was just trying to flower. 'Something's worrying you? Why not tell me about it?' he said.

'Did you love pretty Baby?'

'No, I was accustomed to see him around but he was too small to get interested in and I haven't given him a thought for years. So all's well.'

'There is nothing between us then?'

'Why should there be?'

'Lionel – dare I ask you one more question?'

'Yes, of course.'

'It is about blood. It is the last of all the questions. Have you ever shed blood?'

'No – oh, sorry, I should have said yes. I forgot that little war of mine. It goes clean out of my head between times. A battle's such a mess-up, you wouldn't believe, and this one had a miniature sandstorm raging to make confusion more confounded. Yes, I shed blood all right, or so the official report says. I didn't know at the time.' He was suddenly silent. Vividly and unexpectedly the desert surged up, and he saw it as a cameo, from outside. The central figure – a grotesque one – was himself going berserk, and close to him was a dying savage who had managed to wound him and was trying to speak.

'I hope I never shed blood,' the other said. 'I do not blame others, but for me never.'

'I don't expect you ever will. You're not exactly cut out for a man of war. All the same, I've fallen for you.'

He had not expected to say this, and it was the unexpectedness that so delighted the boy. He turned away his face. It was distorted with joy and suffused with the odd purplish tint that denoted violent emotion. Everything had gone fairly right for a long time. Each step in the stumbling confession had brought him nearer to knowing what the beloved was like. But an open avowal – he had not hoped for so much. 'Before morning I shall have enslaved him,' he thought, 'and he will begin doing whatever I put into his mind.' Even now he did not exult, for he knew by experience that though he always got what he wanted he seldom kept it, also that too much adoration can develop a flaw in the jewel. He remained impassive, crouched like a statue, chin on knees, hands round ankles, waiting for words to which he could safely reply.

'It seemed just a bit of foolery at first,' he went on. 'I woke up properly ashamed of myself after Gib, I don't mind telling you. Since then it's been getting so different, and now it's nothing but us. I tell you one thing though, one silly mistake I've made. I ought never to have mentioned you in that letter to the Mater. There's no advantage in putting her on the scent of something she can't understand; it's all right what we do, I don't mean that.'

'So you want the letter back?'

'But it's posted! Not much use wanting it.'

'Posted?' He was back to his normal and laughed gaily, his sharp teeth gleaming. 'What is posting? Nothing at all, even in a red English pillar box. Even thence you can get most things out, and here is a boat. No! My secretary comes to you tomorrow morning: "Excuse me, Captain March, sir, did you perhaps drop this unposted letter upon the deck?" You thank secretary, you take letter, you write Mater a better letter. Does anything trouble you now?'

'Not really. Except – '

'Except what?'

'Except I'm – I don't know. I'm fonder of you than I know how to say.'

'Should that trouble you?'

O calm mutual night, to one of them triumphant and promising both of them peace! O silence except for the boat bobbing gently! Lionel sighed, with a happiness he couldn't understand. 'You ought to have someone to look after you,' he said tenderly. Had he said this before to a woman and had she responded? No such recollection disturbed him, he did not even know that he was falling in love. 'I wish I could stay with you myself, but of course that's out of the question. If only things were a little different I – come along, let's get our sleep.'

'You shall sleep and you shall awake.' For the moment was upon them at last, the flower opened to receive them, the appointed star mounted the sky, the beloved leaned against him to switch off the light over by the door. He closed his eyes to anticipate divine darkness. He was going to win. All was happening as he had planned, and when morning came and practical life had to be re-entered he would have won.

'Damn!'

The ugly stupid little word rattled out. 'Damn and blast,' Lionel muttered. As he stretched towards the switch, he had noticed the bolt close to it, and he discovered that he had left the door unbolted. The consequences could have been awkward. 'Pretty careless of me,' he reflected, suddenly wide awake. He looked round the cabin as a general might at a battlefield nearly lost by his own folly. The crouched figure was only a unit in it, and no longer the centre of desire. 'Cocoa, I'm awfully sorry,' he went on. 'As a rule it's you who take the risks, this time it's me. I apologise.'

The other roused himself from the twilight where he had hoped to be joined, and tried to follow the meaningless words. Something must have miscarried, but what? The sound of an apology was odious. He had always loathed the English trick of saying 'It's all my fault'; and if he encountered it in business it provided an extra incentive to cheat, and it was contemptible on the lips of a hero. When he grasped what the little trouble was and what the empty 'damns' signified, he closed his eyes again and said, 'Bolt the door therefore.'

'I have.'

'Turn out the light therefore.'

'I will. But a mistake like this makes one feel all insecure. It could have meant a court martial.'

'Could it, man?' he said sadly – sad because the moment towards which they were moving might be passing, because the chances of their convergence might be lost. What could he safely say? 'You was not to blame over the door, dear Lion,' he said. 'I mean we was both to blame. I knew it was unlocked all the time.' He said this hoping to console the beloved and to recall him to the entrance of night. He could not have made a more disastrous remark.

'You knew. But why didn't you say?'

'I had not the time.'

'Not the time to say "Bolt the door"?'

'No, I had not the time. I did not speak because there was no moment for such a speech.'

'No moment when I've been here for ages?'

'And when in that hour? When you come in first? Then? When you embrace me and summon my heart's blood? Is that the moment to speak? When I rest in your arms and you in mine, when our cigarette burns us, when we drink from one glass? When you are smiling? Do I interrupt then? Do I then say "Captain March, sir, you have however forgotten the cabin door"? And when we talk of our faraway boat and of poor pretty Baby whom I never killed and I did not want to kill, and I never dreamt to kill – of what should we talk but of things far away? Lionel, no, no. Lion of the Night, come back to me before our hearts cool. Here is our place and we have so far no other and only we can guard each other. The door shut, the door unshut, is nothing, and is the same.'

'It wouldn't be nothing if the steward had come in,' said Lionel grimly.

'What harm if he did come in?'

'Give him the shock of his life, to say the least of it.'

'No shock at all. Such men are accustomed to far worse. He would be sure of a larger tip and therefore pleased. "Excuse me, gentlemen…" Then he goes and tomorrow my secretary tips him.'

'Cocoa, for God's sake, the things you sometimes say…' The cynicism repelled him. He noticed that it sometimes came after a bout of highfaluting. It was a sort of backwash. 'You never seem to realise the risks we run, either. Suppose I got fired from the Army through this.'

'Yes, suppose?'

'Well, what else could I do?'

'You could be my assistant manager at Basra.'

'Not a very attractive alternative.' He was not sure whether he was being laughed at or not, which always rattled him, and the incident of the unbolted door increased in importance. He apologized again 'for my share in it' and added, 'You've not told that scruffy Parsee about us, I do trust.'

'No. Oh no no no no and oh no. Satisfied?'

'Nor the Goanese steward?'

'Not told. Only tipped. Tip all. Of what other use is money?'

'I shall think you've tipped me next.'

'So I have.'

'That's not a pretty thing to say.'

'I am not pretty. I am not like you.' And he burst into tears. Lionel knew that nerves were on edge, but the suggestion that he was a hireling hurt him badly. He whose pride and duty it was to be independent and command! Had he been regarded as a male prostitute? 'What's upset you?' he said as kindly as possible. 'Don't take on so, Cocoa, there's no occasion for it.'

The sobs continued. He was weeping because he had planned wrongly. Rage rather than grief convulsed him. The bolt unbolted, the little snake not driven back into its hole – he had foreseen everything else and ignored the enemy at the gate.

Bolt and double-bolt now – they would never complete the movement of love. As sometimes happened to him when he was unhinged, he could foretell the immediate future, and he knew before Lionel spoke exactly what he was going to say.

'I think I'll go on deck for a smoke.'

'Go.'

'I've a bit of a headache with this stupid misunderstanding, plus too much booze. I want a breath of fresh air. Then I'll come back.'

'When you come back you will not be you. And I may not be I.'

Further tears. Snivellings. 'We're both to blame,' said Lionel patiently, taking up the cigarette case. 'I'm not letting myself off. I was careless. But why you didn't tell me at once I shall never understand, not if you talk till you're blue. I've explained to you repeatedly that this game we've been playing's a risky one, and honestly I think we'd better never have started it. However, we'll talk about that when you're not so upset.' Here he remembered that the cigarette case was one of his patron's presents to him, so he substituted for it a favourite old pipe. The change was observed and it caused a fresh paroxysm. Like many men of the warm-blooded type, he was sympathetic to a few tears but exasperated when they persisted. Fellow crying and not trying to stop. Fellow crying as if he had the right to cry. Repeating 'I'll come back' as cordially as he could, he went up on deck to think the whole situation over. For there were several things about it he didn't like at all.

Cocoanut stopped weeping as soon as he was alone. Tears were a method of appeal which had failed, and he must seek comfort for his misery and desolation elsewhere. What he longed to do was to climb up into Lionel's berth above him and snuggle down there and dream that he might be joined. He dared not. Whatever else he ventured, it must not be that. It was forbidden to him, although nothing had ever been said. It was the secret place, the sacred place whence strength issued, as he had learned during the first half-hour of the voyage. It was the lair of a beast who might retaliate. So he remained down in his own berth, the safe one, where his lover would certainly never return. It was wiser to work and make money, and he did so for a time. It was still wiser to sleep, and presently he put his ledger aside and lay motionless. His eyes closed. His nostrils occasionally twitched as if responding to something which the rest of his body ignored. The scarf covered him. For it was one of his many superstitions that it is dangerous to lie unclad when alone. Jealous of what she sees, the hag comes with her scimitar, and she… Or she lifts up a man when he feels lighter than air.

5

Up on deck, alone with his pipe, Lionel began to recover his poise and his sense of leadership. Not that he and his pipe were really alone, for the deck was covered with passengers who had had their bedding carried up and now slept under the stars. They lay prone in every direction, and he had to step carefully between them on his way to the railing. He had forgotten that this migration happened nightly as soon as the boat entered the Red Sea; his nights had passed otherwise and elsewhere. Here lay a guileless subaltern, cherry-cheeked; there lay Colonel Arbuthnot, his bottom turned. Mrs Arbuthnot lay parted from her lord in the ladies' section. In the morning, very early, the Goanese stewards would awake the sahibs and carry their bedding back to their cabins. It was an old ritual – not practised in the English Channel or the Bay of Biscay or even in the Mediterranean – and on previous voyages he had taken part in it.

How decent and reliable they looked, the folk to whom he belonged! He had been born one of them, he had his work with them, he meant to marry into their caste. If he forfeited their companionship he would become nobody and nothing. The widened expanse of the sea, the winking lighthouse, helped to compose him, but what really recalled him to sanity was this quiet sleeping company of his peers. He liked his profession, and was rising in it thanks to that little war; it would be mad to jeopardise it, which he had been doing ever since he drank too much champagne at Gibraltar.

Not that he had ever been a saint. No – he had occasionally joined a brothel expedition, so as not to seem better than his fellow officers. But he had not been so much bothered by sex as were some of them. He hadn't had the time, what with his soldiering duties and his obligations at home as eldest son, and the doc said an occasional wet dream was nothing to worry about. Don't sleep on your back, though. On this simple routine he had proceeded since puberty. And during the past few months he had proceeded even further. Learning that he was to be posted to India, where he would contact Isabel, he had disciplined himself more severely and had practised chastity even in thought. It was the least he could do for the girl he hoped to marry. Sex had entirely receded – only to come charging back like a bull. That infernal Cocoa – the mischief he had done. He had woken up so much that might have slept.

For Isabel's sake, as for his profession's, their foolish relationship must stop at once. He could not think how he had yielded to it, or why it had involved him so deeply. It would have ended at Bombay, it would have to end now, and Cocoanut must cry his eyes out if he thought it worthwhile. So far all was clear. But behind Isabel, behind the Army, was another power, whom he could not consider calmly: his mother, blind-eyed in the midst of the enormous web she had spun – filaments drifting everywhere, strands catching. There was no reasoning with her or about her, she understood nothing and controlled everything. She had suffered too much and was too high-minded to be judged like other people, she was outside carnality and incapable of pardoning it. Earlier in the evening, when Cocoa mentioned her, he had tried to imagine her with his father, enjoying the sensations he was beginning to find so pleasant, but the attempt was sacrilegious and he was shocked at himself. From the great blank country she inhabited came a voice condemning him and all her children for sin, but condemning him most. There was no parleying with her – she was a voice. God had not granted her ears – nor could she see, mercifully: the sight of him stripping would have killed her. He, her first-born, set apart for the redemption of the family name. His surviving brother was too much a bookworm to be of any use, and the other two were girls.

He spat into the sea. He promised her 'Never again'. The words went out into the night like other enchantments. He said them aloud, and Colonel Arbuthnot, who was a light sleeper, woke up and switched on his torch.

'Hullo, who's that, what's there?'

'March, sir, Lionel March. I'm afraid I've disturbed you.'

'No, no, Lionel, that's all right, I wasn't asleep. Ye gods, what gorgeous pyjamas the fellow's wearing. What's he going about like a lone wolf for? Eh?'

'Too hot in my cabin, sir. Nothing sinister.'

'How goes the resident wog?'

'The resident wog he sleeps.'

'By the way, what's his name?'

'Moraes, I believe.'

'Exactly. Mr Moraes is in for trouble.'

'Oh. What for, sir?'

'For being on board. Lady Manning has just heard the story. It turns out that he gave someone in the London office a fat bribe to get him a passage though the boat was full, and as an easy way out they put him into your cabin. I don't care who gives or takes bribes. Doesn't interest me. But if the Company thinks it can treat a British officer like that it's very much mistaken. I'm going to raise hell at Bombay.'

'He's not been any particular nuisance,' said Lionel after a pause.

'I daresay not. It's the question of our prestige in the East, and it's also very hard luck on you, very hard. Why don't you come and sleep on deck like the rest of the gang?'

'Sound idea. I will.'

'We've managed to cordon off this section of the deck, and woe betide anything black that walks this way, if it's only a beetle. Good night.'

'Good night, sir.' Then something snapped and he heard himself shouting, 'Bloody rubbish, leave the kid alone.'

'Wh – what's that, didn't catch,' said the puzzled Colonel.

'Nothing sir, sorry sir.' And he was back in the cabin.

Why on earth had he nearly betrayed himself just as everything was going right? There seemed a sort of devil around. At the beginning of the voyage he had tempted him to throw himself overboard for no reason, but this was something more serious. 'When you come back to the cabin you will not be you,' Cocoa had said; and was it so?

However, the lower berth was empty, that was something, the boy must have gone to the lav, and he slipped out of his effeminate pyjamas and prepared to finish the night where he belonged – a good sleep there would steady him. His forearm was already along the rail, his foot poised for the upspring, when he saw what had happened.

'Hullo, Cocoanut, up in my berth for a change?' he said in clipped officer-tones, for it was dangerous to get angry. 'Stay there if you want to, I've just decided to sleep on deck.' There was no reply, but his own remarks pleased him and he decided to go further. 'As a matter of fact I shan't be using our cabin again except when it is absolutely necessary,' he continued. 'It's scarcely three days to Bombay, so I can easily manage, and I shan't, we shan't be meeting again after disembarkation. As I said earlier on, the whole thing has been a bit of a mistake. I wish we...' He stopped. If only it wasn't so difficult to be kind! But his talk with the Colonel and his communion with the Mater prevented it. He must keep with his own people, or he would perish. He added, 'Sorry to have to say all this.'

'Kiss me.'

The words fell quietly after his brassiness and vulgarity and he could not answer them. The face was close to his now, the body curved away seductively into darkness.

'Kiss me.'

'No.'

'Noah? No? Then I kiss you.' And he lowered his mouth on to the muscular forearm and bit it.

Lionel yelped with pain.

'Bloody bitch, wait till I...' Blood oozed between the gold-bright hairs. 'You wait...' And the scar in his groin reopened. The cabin vanished. He was back in a desert fighting savages. One of them asked for mercy, stumbled, and found none.

The sweet act of vengeance followed, sweeter than ever for both of them, and as ecstasy hardened into agony his hands twisted the throat. Neither of them knew when the end came, and he when he realised it felt no sadness, no remorse. It was part of a curve that had long been declining, and had nothing to do with death. He covered again with his warmth and kissed the closed eyelids tenderly and spread the bright-coloured scarf. Then he burst out of the stupid cabin on to the deck, and naked and with the seeds of love on him he dived into the sea.

The scandal was appalling. The Big Eight did their best, but it was soon all over the boat that a British officer had committed suicide after murdering a half-caste. Some of the passengers recoiled from such news. Others snuffled for more. The secretary of Moraes was induced to gossip and hint at proclivities, the cabin steward proved to have been over-tipped, the Master at Arms had had complaints which he had managed to stifle, the Purser had been suspicious throughout, and the doctor who examined the injuries divulged that strangulation was only one of them, and that March had been a monster in human form, of whom the earth was well rid. The cabin was sealed up for further examination later, and the place where the two boys had made love and the tokens they had exchanged in their love went on without them to Bombay. For Lionel had been only a boy.

His body was never recovered – the blood on it quickly attracted the sharks. The body of his victim was consigned to the deep with all possible speed. There was a slight disturbance at the funeral. The native crew had become interested in it, no one understood why, and when the corpse was lowered were heard betting which way it would float. It moved northwards – contrary to the prevailing current – and there were clappings of hands and some smiles.

Finally Mrs March had to be informed. Colonel Arbuthnot and Lady Manning were deputed for the thankless task. Colonel Arbuthnot assured her that her son's death had been accidental, whatever she heard to the contrary; that he had stumbled overboard in the darkness during a friendly talk they had had together on deck. Lady Manning spoke with warmth and affection of his good looks and good manners and his patience 'with us old fogies at our Bridge'. Mrs March thanked them for writing but made no comment. She also received a letter from Lionel himself – the one that should have been intercepted in the post – and she never mentioned his name again.

Notes

1. 'Madam – madam, I am hungry' (French).
2. 'Did you not invite me to tea?' (French).
3. Victorious virgin (Latin).
4. Virgil, *Aeneid*, VI, l. 122, 'again and again he journeys back and forth' (Latin).
5. Virgil, *Georgics*, III, l. 281, 'the slimy fluid oozes from his groin' (Latin).

Biographical note

Edward Morgan Forster was born in London in 1879 to Edward Forster, an architect, and Alice Whichelo. He was educated at Tonbridge School and then went on to King's College, Cambridge, where he met many members of the future Bloomsbury Group. He retained a lifelong association with King's College and was elected to an Honorary Fellowship in 1946.

On leaving Cambridge in 1901, Forster travelled through Europe for a year; his experiences and observations of his fellow-tourists providing material for his early novels. Once back in England, he began writing for the newly launched *Independent Review*, and in 1905 he completed his first novel, *Where Angels Fear to Tread*. This was followed by *The Longest Journey* (1907), *A Room with a View* (1908), and *Howards End* (1910). By now he was firmly established as a writer of considerable importance.

In 1912 he visited India, and the ensuing *A Passage to India* (1924) was awarded the Prix Femina Vie Heureuse and the James Tait Black Memorial Prize. This was to be his last novel; *Maurice*, which was written in 1913, was not published until after his death, in 1971. Instead, Forster devoted his life to a range of literary activities, notably his strong stance against censorship. His famous work of literary criticism *Aspects of the Novel* appeared in 1927, and by this time he was regularly lecturing at Cambridge. He also penned a collection of essays, a biography, and, with Eric Crozier, the libretto for Benjamin Britten's *Billy Budd* (1951). Upon his death in 1970, *The Times* hailed him as among 'the most esteemed English novelists of his time'.

HESPERUS PRESS

Hesperus Press, as suggested by the Latin motto, is committed to bringing near what is far – far both in space and time. Works written by the greatest authors, and unjustly neglected or simply little known in the English-speaking world, are made accessible through new translations and a completely fresh editorial approach. Through these classic works, the reader is introduced to the greatest writers from all times and all cultures.

For more information on Hesperus Press, please visit our website: **www.hesperuspress.com**

ET REMOTISSIMA PROPE

MODERN VOICES

SELECTED TITLES FROM HESPERUS PRESS

Author	Title	Foreword writer
Mikhail Bulgakov	*A Dog's Heart*	A.S. Byatt
Mikhail Bulgakov	*The Fatal Eggs*	Doris Lessing
Anthony Burgess	*The Eve of St Venus*	
Colette	*Claudine's House*	Doris Lessing
Marie Ferranti	*The Princess of Mantua*	
Beppe Fenoglio	*A Private Affair*	Paul Bailey
F. Scott Fitzgerald	*The Popular Girl*	Helen Dunmore
F. Scott Fitzgerald	*The Rich Boy*	John Updike
Graham Greene	*No Man's Land*	David Lodge
Franz Kafka	*Metamorphosis*	Martin Jarvis
Franz Kafka	*The Trial*	Zadie Smith
D.H. Lawrence	*Wintry Peacock*	Amit Chaudhuri
Rosamond Lehmann	*The Gipsy's Baby*	Niall Griffiths
Carlo Levi	*Words are Stones*	Anita Desai
André Malraux	*The Way of the Kings*	Rachel Seiffert
Katherine Mansfield	*In a German Pension*	Linda Grant
Katherine Mansfield	*Prelude*	William Boyd
Vladimir Mayakovsky	*My Discovery of America*	Colum McCann
Luigi Pirandello	*Loveless Love*	
Françoise Sagan	*The Unmade Bed*	
Jean-Paul Sartre	*The Wall*	Justin Cartwright
Bernard Shaw	*The Adventures of the Black Girl in Her Search for God*	Colm Tóibín
Georges Simenon	*Three Crimes*	
Leonard Woolf	*A Tale Told by Moonlight*	Victoria Glendinning
Virginia Woolf	*Memoirs of a Novelist*	